F00

SPECIAL MESSAGE TO READERS

THE ULVERSCROFT FOUNDATION
(registered UK charity number 264873)

was established in 1972 to provide funds for research, diagnosis and treatment of eye diseases. Examples of major projects funded by the Ulverscroft Foundation are:-

- The Children's Eye Unit at Moorfields Eye Hospital, London
- The Ulverscroft Children's Eye Unit at Great Ormond Street Hospital for Sick Children
- Funding research into eye diseases and treatment at the Department of Ophthalmology, University of Leicester
- The Ulverscroft Vision Research Group, Institute of Child Health
- Twin operating theatres at the Western Ophthalmic Hospital, London
- The Chair of Ophthalmology at the Royal Australian College of Ophthalmologists

You can help further the work of the Foundation by making a donation or leaving a legacy. Every contribution is gratefully received. If you would like to help support the Foundation or require further information, please contact:

THE ULVERSCROFT FOUNDATION
The Green, Bradgate Road, Anstey
Leicester LE7 7FU, England
Tel: (0116) 236 4325
website: www.foundation.ulverscroft.com

THE WITCHES' MOON

Mr. Dench left his house on a wet September night to post a letter at a nearby pillar-box — and disappeared. A fortnight later his dead body was found in a tunnel a few miles away. He had been brutally murdered. Called in to investigate, Superintendent Robert Budd soon realizes that Dench hadn't planned to disappear. But it's not until he finds the secret of the fireman's helmet, the poetic pickpocket, and the Witches' Moon that he discovers why Mr. Dench — and several other people — have been murdered . . .

GERALD VERNER

THE WITCHES' MOON

Complete and Unabridged

LINFORD
Leicester

First published in Great Britain

First Linford Edition
published 2016

A catalogue record for this book is available
from the British Library.

ISBN 978–1–4448–2701–9

Published by
F. A. Thorpe (Publishing)
Anstey, Leicestershire

Set by Words & Graphics Ltd.
Anstey, Leicestershire
Printed and bound in Great Britain by
T. J. International Ltd., Padstow, Cornwall

This book is printed on acid-free paper

1

The Vanishing Man

Mr. James Augustus Dench was unknown to the general public until he walked out of his small, neat villa in Ebury Avenue, King's Mailing, to post a letter and never came back.

He left his house at ten o'clock on a wet September night attired in an old lounge suit, a shabby pair of leather slippers, and a cloth cap. The pillar-box which was his ostensible objective was barely a hundred yards away from his gate, and the fact that he reached it was proved later, for the letter which he had taken with him to post arrived at its destination on the following morning. Whatever happened, therefore, to Mr. Dench must have occurred on his return journey.

The police who were subsequently called in explored every possible field of inquiry, but without discovering any explanation for the missing man's mysterious disappearance.

He had lived with his sister in a modest, unassuming way, and possessed few friends. There was nothing in his past or present that offered the remotest motive for his sudden and unaccountable absence.

The police, having exhausted every conceivable hypothesis, fell back on the 'loss of memory' theory, though it certainly seemed incredible that such a catastrophe could have overtaken a man within the short time necessary to cover the small distance between the house and the post-box.

One thing was obvious, and that was that Mr. Dench had not set out with the intention of never returning. The fact that he was dressed in slippers and, although it was a wet night, had taken no overcoat, proved this.

His description was circulated all over the country and an SOS broadcast was sent out by the British Broadcasting Corporation. But none of these had the effect of producing any news of the missing Mr.

Dench, and it was not until nearly three weeks had elapsed that any trace of him was discovered. And then he reappeared in circumstances that were as mysterious as those surrounding his disappearance.

Some workmen engaged in repairs to a tunnel at Seldon Cutting, near Mallington Junction, the nearest station to Kings Mailing, found in an alcove, about two hundred yards from the mouth of the tunnel, the doubled-up body of a man. The body was covered with soot and grime, and from its appearance had obviously been dead for some time. The police were notified of the discovery immediately, and an examination showed that the man had met his death by a knife wound in the back. A search of the pockets revealed nothing to indicate his identity, but from his clothes and the fact that he was wearing leather slippers they came to the conclusion that the body was that of Mr. James Augustus Dench, and that he had been murdered.

To the annoyance of Inspector Tipman, who had been in charge of the inquiries concerning Mr. Dench's disappearance, the chief constable of the county, when the murder was reported to him, insisted on calling in the assistance of Scotland Yard. The letter which he wrote was passed for attention to the assistant-commissioner, Colonel Blair, who read it, and immediately sent for Superintendent Robert Budd. As a result of the brief interview which followed, that big, sleepy-eyed man, accompanied by Sergeant Leek, set off in his ancient and dingy little car for Kings Mailing, heralded by an official telegram notifying Inspector Tipman of his arrival.

Kings Mailing is neither a village nor a town, neither completely rural nor completely urban. It is a mixture of both, as though, having suddenly made up its mind to acquire the full dignity of township, it had lost ambition halfway and remained in an indeterminate middle state. On the outskirts there are several thatched cottages and one or two straggling farms — relics of the days when it was definitely a village. Rows of new villas and shops testify to its unsuccessful efforts to reach a more pretentious position on the map.

It nestled cosily in a hollow with the

rising slope of the Berkshire Hills behind it. There is no railway station at Kings Mailing itself, the nearest being Mallington Junction, some two and a half miles distant. The road to the junction is a continuation of the High Street and runs in a wide curve through open country. There used to be, when Kings Mailing was a village, an inn on this road — a rather picturesque old place with white stone walls and leaded windows, the thatched roof and oak beams so low that the unwary might bump their heads. The inn is still there, but to its name, the Crooked Compasses, has been added the glorification of 'Hotel.' The thatched roof has been replaced by very new red tiles; the leaded windows by plain glass; the old stone by yellow brickwork.

Nothing remains of the original building but the oak beams, and these have been enhanced by much pseudo-Jacobean furniture and pewter-work from Birmingham.

It stands close to the road, and shows up rather glaringly against the background of ancient trees which, beginning as a thin copse, develops into a dense wood. Mr. Budd saw this unbeautiful building as he came round a bend in the road, and brought his dilapidated machine to a halt at the entrance.

A thick-set man who had been standing at the door came towards him as he began to extricate himself with difficulty from the driving seat. 'Superintendent Budd?' he inquired.

'That's me,' said the big man.

'I'm Inspector Tipman,' said the florid-faced man in a business-like tone. 'I received your telegram arranging that I should meet you here, though I should have thought the police station would have been more suitable.'

'More suitable but not so comfortable,' murmured Mr. Budd gently. 'My experience of police stations, Inspector, is that there's no decent chair in which one can sit with any degree of ease. Naturally there's a lot we've got to talk about, and I thought we might do it under the most pleasant conditions.'

'As you like,' said the inspector a little stiffly. 'Shall we go inside?'

Mr. Budd nodded, suppressing a yawn. 'May as well,' he answered. 'What's the beer like here?'

'This is the first time I've ever been inside the place,' replied Tipman shortly.

'Oh, well,' said the big man, 'we'll have to chance it then, I suppose. Funny thing, when you come to think of it, what a lot of difference there is in beer. Some's good, some's middlin', and some's undrinkable. Let's hope we're lucky.'

Accompanied by the lugubrious Leek, he followed the inspector into a low-ceilinged lounge which, except for themselves, was completely deserted. 'Let's sit over here,' he said, moving ponderously towards a table in the far corner. 'We can talk without bein' overheard, and in comfort.'

Tipman acquiesced in silence, and to judge from the expression on his face, was not altogether impressed by either the habits or the appearance of his London colleague. Mr. Budd settled himself in a wicker armchair, which uttered a protesting squeak under his weight, and looked round sleepily. 'What'll you have?' he asked as he caught the eye of an aged waiter who was hovering about expectantly.

'I'd rather you excused me,' said Inspector Tipman primly. 'I make it a habit never to drink on duty.'

The superintendent shook his head with a grimace. 'You're nearly as bad as my sergeant,' he remarked sorrowfully. 'He only drinks lime juice. That's why he's got such a sour face. Have somethin', man, if it's only a lemonade.'

'Very well, if you insist, I'll have a dry ginger,' replied the inspector, conveying by his tone that he was making a great concession.

Mr Budd raised his eyes to the decrepit waiter who had hobbled over to the table and was standing hopefully. 'A pint of bitter, a small lime juice, and a dry ginger,' he said gently. 'And let's have the beer in a tankard, if you can.'

The man went to fetch the order, and Mr. Budd, extracting a thin black cigar from his waistcoat pocket, lit it carefully and slowly blew out a cloud of rank smoke. Sergeant Leek who, up to now had remained silent, ventured a remark.

'I remember now,' he said suddenly.

'Oh, you do, eh?' grunted his superior. 'Well, that's somethin'. What do you remember?'

'I've been tryin' to recollect,' said Leek, 'when we was down here before, and now I remember. It was over the Marsh business.'

Mr. Budd frowned. 'Why bring that up?' he answered shortly.

Although three years had elapsed since the murder of Hebert Marsh at the big house on the outskirts of Kings Mailing, he was still a little sore on the subject, for it represented one of his few failures, and still rankled.

'I was only thinkin',' began Leek apologetically.

'Well, don't!' snapped Mr. Budd severely.

The waiter shuffled up with the drinks, and when he had paid for them the superintendent sampled the contents of his tankard. 'Ah!' he said with relish, smacking his lips. 'That's what I call beer!' He took a long draught, set the tankard down, and leaned back in his chair with a sigh of contentment. 'Now, Inspector,' he murmured, 'let's hear all about this Dench business.'

Inspector Tipman cleared his throat, produced from an inside pocket a black-covered notebook, and began a recital of the events which had led up to the discovery of Mr. Dench's body in the tunnel at Seldon Cutting.

The superintendent listened with closed eyes, although as far as outward appearances went he seemed to have fallen asleep. He made no comment until Tipman had finished, and then he opened his eyes wearily. 'Interestin' and peculiar,' he murmured. 'And queer. I suppose there's no doubt that the dead man found in the tunnel *was* Dench?'

The inspector eyed him, a little startled. 'Not the slightest,' he replied. 'The body has been identified by his sister, and the clothes, even to his slippers, are the same he was wearing when he disappeared.'

'They prove nothin',' said Mr. Budd. 'Identification by the sister, however, seems fairly conclusive, though by no means definitely so.'

'Are you suggesting — ' began Tipman, but the other interrupted him.

'I'm not suggestin' anythin',' he said. 'But when you're inquiring into a murder it's just as well to know whose murder it is you're inquirin' into.' He leaned forward, picked up his tankard, and drained the remainder of its contents at a gulp.

'Well,' he said with a sigh, 'I suppose we'd better be gettin' started. Where have they taken the body?'

'To the mortuary at Mallington,' answered Tipman.

'Then,' said the superintendent, hoisting himself ponderously to his feet, 'that's where I want to start.'

★   ★   ★

Inspector Tipman drew back the sheet, and Mr. Budd bent over the thing that lay on the cold stone slab. It was not a pleasant sight, for time and the grime of the tunnel had combined to obliterate almost any resemblance to a human being; and, accustomed as he was to these

11

sights, the stout man could scarcely suppress a slight shudder as he looked at this grotesque travesty of what had once been a man.

'He looks to have been dead a long time,' he remarked. 'Post-mortem staining is very advanced.'

'According to the doctor's evidence,' Tipman said, 'he must have been dead at least a week.'

'And you say that he's been definitely identified by his sister?' asked Mr. Budd.

'Yes,' the inspector answered, 'and without any hesitation whatever.'

The big man glanced once more at the marble slab bathed in the hard white rays of the unshaded bulb that hung over it. 'I don't see how she could have been so certain,' he grunted, frowning. 'I should have thought the condition of the body made identification pretty difficult.'

'Ordinarily you'd be right,' said Tipman, 'but you see in this case Miss Dench had two things to help her — that star-shaped scar which you can see on the dead man's chin and the little toe of the right foot, which is missing. Both these things were characteristics of her brother.'

'I see,' said Mr. Budd, nodding several times. 'Yes, of course, that 'ud make a difference.'

He began a close examination of the body while Leek and the inspector stood and watched him in silence. After a little while he looked up. 'Notice this?' he said, pointing to the thin wrists. 'These marks here. There are several scratches and bruises. What do you make of them?'

'I put them down as a result of a struggle with the man who killed him,' said Tipman.

The superintendent shook his head doubtfully. 'I think you're wrong there,' he murmured. 'If they were only on his wrists your explanation might be right. But if you look closely at his ankles you'll find that the marks are repeated there, too, though in a much lesser degree.'

The local man lowered his head and peered in the direction of Mr. Budd's chubby finger. 'Yes, I can see 'em now you mention it,' he said. 'But they're very faint. How did you manage to spot 'em?'

'I spotted 'em,' replied Mr. Budd

slowly, 'because I was lookin' for 'em.'

The inspector stared at him in astonishment. 'D'you mean you expected to find them?'

'I expected somethin' of the sort,' replied the other. 'And if you take the trouble to think for a moment you'll see why. Here's a fellow who leaves his house one evenin' to post a letter and completely disappears. Three weeks later his dead body is found in a tunnel within two miles of his home. He's obviously been murdered, and accordin' to the doctor has been dead for over a week when he was found. The question that comes naturally is, what happened to him between the time he disappeared and the time he met his death and was placed in the tunnel? It's pretty obvious, from what we know, that he didn't disappear of his own free will. Therefore, durin' those two weeks he must have been held by a third person, or persons. Now, the simplest way to keep a prisoner is to tie him up so he can't move. Now do you see why I was lookin' for marks on his wrists and ankles?'

'That's all right as far as it goes,' Tipman assented dubiously, 'but we've got no evidence that Dench didn't disappear of his own free will.'

'Oh yes we have,' answered Mr. Budd. 'His clothes. No man who had made up his mind to disappear 'ud choose to do so wearin' slippers and without a hat. He wouldn't be able to get very far without attractin' attention in that rig-out, and that would be the very thing he would wish to avoid.'

Rather reluctantly the inspector was forced to agree. 'All the same,' he grunted, 'I don't see how it's going to help us.'

'I think it's going to help us quite a lot,' said Mr. Budd thoughtfully, 'because it tells us somethin' else. It tells us that he was kept prisoner somewhere in the district.'

'I don't see how you get that,' muttered the inspector.

'Because,' explained Mr. Budd patiently, 'there'd have been no point in hidin' the body in the tunnel if they'd had to bring it very far. It would have been risky takin' it further than was necessary. And there can have been no particular object in choosin' the tunnel except that it offered a good hidin' place within easy reach.'

'Then you think the place where Dench was killed is somewhere near Seldon Cutting?' said Tipman.

'Yes, I do,' agreed Mr. Budd. 'I'm pretty sure of it. Was any weapon found?'

'No,' said Tipman, shaking his head. 'But the doctor says that a rather broad-bladed knife was used. From the bruising of the flesh round the wound he suggests a large clasp knife with a short blade.'

'H'm! I should like to look at his clothes,' said the superintendent.

The inspector went over to a plain wooden cupboard in one corner of the bare whitewashed room, and taking a key from his pocket unlocked it. From a shelf he took an armful of clothes, and bringing them back put them on a chair by the side of the marble slab. Mr. Budd picked them up one by one and sleepily inspected them. They were stained and indescribably dirty. The smoke and soot of the tunnel had ingrained itself into the cloth, and apart from that there were traces of mud and some peculiar yellowish specks which he could not place at first, but which he eventually decided were particles of sawdust.

He looked at this more closely and found that it was not new. It had a discoloured, seasoned appearance. The back of the coat was stiff with blood round the narrow slit where the knife had entered; so were the waistcoat and shirt. The pockets were empty, and evidently had been hurriedly rifled, for the breast pocket of the jacket and the hip pocket of the trousers were turned completely inside out.

Apart from the specks of sawdust, however, there was nothing, and he turned his attention to the slippers. The soles of these were caked with mud, in which was embedded several blades of grass and a rather larger quantity of sawdust. He pointed this out to Tipman.

'It may help us to find the place we're lookin' for,' he said. 'It's unusual to find sawdust in an ordinary house, and obviously he's been in a place with sawdust.

It's on his clothes as well.'

'I noticed that,' Tipman said with a frown. 'But I didn't think it was important.'

'Maybe it isn't,' said Mr. Budd. 'Maybe it is. You never can tell. What was Dench?'

'He'd retired,' answered the inspector, 'but he used to be the foreman with a firm of safe-makers in Stepney.'

'Oh, he did.' The superintendent gently caressed his cascade of chins. 'Foreman to a firm of safe-makers. Now that's interestin'.' Before Inspector Tipman could inquire why it was interesting, the big man had gone off on another track.

'I'd like to have a word with the sister,' he said. 'There's nothin' more we can do here at the moment.'

They left the little mortuary and went out to his waiting car. Ebury Avenue, Mr. Budd discovered when they reached it, was not really an avenue at all, for there were no trees except those which grew in the back gardens of the small, red-roofed houses that lined either side of the street. These were so like each other that they gave an impression of having been turned out of one gigantic mould and deposited side by side in a row. Each was red-roofed; each was covered with white stucco; each possessed an ornate affair of oak which covered the narrow, green-painted front door. Each had hanging from this structure a small, square, wrought-iron lamp, and each was set in a parallelogram of garden enclosed by low brick walls, from the top of which protruded oak posts strung together with chains.

Number twenty-nine, from which on that wet September night Mr. James Augustus Dench had gone forth never to return, differed not in the slightest respect from its neighbours, and the only thing that served to mark it out from the rest of the avenue was the colour of the curtains in the windows, which were a bright and rather unpleasant shade of blue.

The superintendent brought his little car to a halt and got down. In answer to their ring the front door was opened by an elderly woman with rather frizzy grey hair. Her thin face was haggard and still bore traces of recent grief.

'I'm sorry to bother you again, ma'am,' said Inspector Tipman politely, 'but this is Superintendent Budd, of Scotland Yard, who has come down to inquire into the murder of your brother.'

'Please come in,' said the woman in a low voice, and ushered them into a rather old-fashioned sitting room.

'I shan't detain you long, ma'am,' said Mr. Budd, 'but there's just one or two questions I'd like to put to you.'

'Anything I can do to help find the person who was responsible for James's death I am only too willing,' she said, and there was a hard note in her voice. 'It's a dreadful thing! A dreadful thing!'

'How long had you and your brother been living in this district, ma'am?' Mr. Budd asked gently.

'Nearly three years,' she answered. 'We came here when James retired.'

'He was employed, I understand,' said the big man, 'by a firm of safe-makers in Stepney?'

'Yes, that's quite right,' she said.

'Could you give me the name of the firm?' he went on.

'The Leyland Safe Company Limited, Ponders Road, Stepney,' she answered promptly.

Mr. Budd took a notebook from his pocket and laboriously wrote it down. 'I suppose,' he continued, 'it's useless askin' you if you can suggest any motive for the murder?'

'Quite!' she declared. 'The police have already asked me that, but I can think of nothing. James was a very quiet, inoffensive man. He was fond of his garden and an occasional game of billiards. There was nothing, so far as I know, for which any person could have wished his death.'

'He was never concerned with any trial or criminal proceedings?' said the big man, and she shook her head.

'No, not to my knowledge,' she answered.

'Had he always lived with you, ma'am?' asked the superintendent.

'Yes,' she replied. 'I've always looked after him.'

'Where did you live before you came here?'

'In Stepney. 18, Harwell Road.'

21

He made a note of her answer. 'Now, ma'am,' he said, 'I think that's all I've got to worry you about, except that I'd like to have a look through your brother's effects, if you don't mind.'

'We've already done so,' put in Inspector Tipman, 'but there was nothing.'

'Well, it won't hurt to have another look,' said Mr. Budd. 'Two heads are better than one, and therefore four eyes must be better than two.' He rose ponderously to his feet. 'I'm obliged to you, ma'am. No, don't trouble to come with us,' he added as the woman made a movement. 'Inspector Tipman knows the way.'

In the company of the openly impatient Tipman he made an exhaustive search, and it was in the dead man's bedroom that his diligence was partially rewarded. By the side of the fireplace was a cupboard containing a number of suits and other items of apparel, and in the jacket pocket of an old, discarded blue serge the big man came upon a scrap of dingy paper. On it were three words scrawled in faint pencil ' — Marsh

Wildcroft Manor.'

Mr. Budd deciphered them with difficulty and frowned. The suit was ancient, the paper old and dirty, but — Hebert Marsh had been murdered and his murderer had never been found. Was there any connection between that three-year-old crime and the death of Dench?

It was worth considering. Perhaps in seeking a solution of the latter he would find an explanation for the former. It was only a vague possibility when it first occurred to him, but in the light of later events he realized just *how* right his instinct had been.

2

Wildcroft Manor

The Marsh case was almost a classic, one of the few which the police had failed to solve. The murderer of Hebert Marsh was still at large somewhere. He had never been caught, and neither had any motive for the crime come to light.

He had been shot dead in his bedroom at Wildcroft Manor, the big house on the outskirts of Kings Mailing, where he was entertaining a weekend house party. He had been shot squarely between the eyes, and apparently the crime had been committed just as he was preparing to go to bed, for when the body was found the feet were bare, and it was dressed only in pyjamas. One of the most extraordinary features of the crime was the fact that the bedroom window and all the other windows in the house were tightly fastened, and the doors chained and bolted. So the killer could not have come from the outside — a fact which was further borne out by the fog, which, according to the statements of the guests taken at the time, had come up with nightfall and remained throughout the greater part of the following day.

The shot that had killed Marsh had been plainly heard by everybody, and the body had been discovered within three minutes of its decease. The general conclusion had been that the murderer was among the guests whom the dead man had collected around him for that fatal weekend. But there was nothing to connect any of them with the crime, and after a long and tedious investigation the police had been reluctantly compelled to admit themselves baffled, and had allowed the affair to drop into the category of unsolved mysteries.

The result might have been different if Scotland Yard had been called in at once, but the local police had allowed a fortnight to elapse before asking for the assistance of their London colleagues; and when Mr. Budd, who had been put in charge of the case, had arrived, the scent was cold and any clues there might have been, obliterated. It was one of his few failures, and although three years had elapsed the memory of it still rankled. It had been before Inspector Tipman's time, and one of the last investigations which poor old Branscombe had handled before pneumonia had cut short his life.

Tipman was not impressed with the big man's discovery. He was a little annoyed that it had been overlooked in the previous search, but he obviously considered it unimportant. And Mr. Budd kept his idea that there might be a connection between the two crimes to himself. Wildcroft Manor had been shut up since the murder of its owner, and he was wondering if that empty and rambling mansion might not hold the secret of James Augustus Dench's hiding place between the time of his disappearance and his death.

He was silent and preoccupied when they left the house in Ebury Avenue and rejoined Leek, who had been left in the car. Inspector Tipman had arranged an appointment with the chief constable for that afternoon, and after a modest lunch Mr. Budd presented himself at the police station at Mallington.

Colonel Walling he had met before, on his previous visit: a typical retired army man, conscientious, a stickler for routine and *esprit de corps*, but not gifted with a great deal of imagination. The conference, which took up the greater part of the afternoon, was, in the big man's opinion, purely a waste of time, and led to no useful results.

He listened sleepily to everything the chief constable had to say and to Inspector Tipman's comments. But his mind was more occupied with the nebulous suggestion which the discovery of that scrap of paper in Dench's discarded suit had offered, and by the time the consultation came to an end he had reached a decision. Lodgings had been obtained for himself and Leek at the cottage belonging to the station sergeant, and when their bags had been deposited and he had had a wash, he set off to put this into execution, leaving the melancholy Leek to his own devices.

It was dark when he started, but he knew every inch of the way as well as he knew the back of his own hand. He had decided, much as he disliked walking, to go on foot.

Leaving the lane in which the cottage was situated, he turned to the right, which led him into a narrow road that eventually brought him to another winding lane along which it would have been impossible to drive the car. Halfway down this was a stile, and laboriously climbing it, Mr. Budd turned off onto a footpath which ran through a thick wood.

The track was rough and scarcely discernible in the gloom of the coming night, and he was forced to slacken his pace. While he zigzagged his way among the trees he ran over in his mind the circumstances surrounding the disappearance and death of Dench.

The whole thing, of course, turned on the motive. Why had Dench been kidnapped in the first place? And why had his abductors kept him a prisoner? If his murder was necessary to their plans, why hadn't they killed him at once instead of waiting for nearly a week? There seemed to be only one answer to this. Dench was in possession of, or knew of, something that they wanted, and until they had succeeded in squeezing that information out of him they had kept him alive. But what was the something? Could it have anything to do with the murder of Hebert Marsh? Mr. Budd thought it was quite likely, but he could think of no satisfactory theory to link the two crimes.

The straggling path along which he was walking now began to widen and the trees to thin out. He came to another stile, and crossing a narrow cart track plunged into a thick wood on the other side of which was an eerie group of trees, known locally as the 'birdless copse'.

It was quite dark by now, and the night was very still. A slither of bright, hard moon had risen, shining through the frosty air like burnished silver. A few hundred yards farther on the trees ended abruptly and, divided by a strip of rank grass, ran along the old post road. Its surface was broken and rutted; clumps of weeds covered it, and it had evidently not been used as a thoroughfare for some considerable time.

The superintendent moved into the shadow of a high wall of crumbling brick to which the ivy clung in a mantle of dark green. He followed the wall until it turned at right angles, and presently came upon the gates of Wildcroft Manor. Inside the dark drive, with its avenue of poplars, stood the deserted lodge, its windows shuttered from within. The gates were of wrought iron, fastened by a padlock and chain.

Mr. Budd muttered an imprecation. He ought to have expected that. The house was neither to let or for sale, merely in disuse. Probably the furniture was still there. Of course the gates would be kept locked!

And then, as he shook them gently, the chain fell apart and dropped, with the padlock, at his feet. Stooping, he picked it up, and his eyes narrowed as he saw that one of the links had been filed. Some unauthorised person had been there, and recently. The edges of the broken links were still bright.

He opened one of the gates sufficiently to squeeze himself through and stood on the weed-covered drive. The avenue of poplars looked dark and uninviting. There was no sign of life; no sound broke the intense stillness that brooded over the place like an invisible shroud. He felt in his pocket to assure himself that his torch was there, and moved slowly up the approach.

The house came into view: a big, rambling mansion of white stone covered with patches of ivy and creeper. It was a gloomy, forbidding-looking building which the silver moonlight seemed, in some indefinable way, to render sinister. On every hand were signs of neglect and disuse. The flowerbed and the lawn were a riot of weeds and rank grass. A broken pergola, stretching away to the rose garden, was a mass of trailing briars. The sightless windows stared like the eyes of a dead thing.

Mr. Budd was not an imaginative man, but he gave a little shiver. Here, three years before, a man had been killed and his killer had gone unpunished. Here, perhaps, if his theory was right, James Augustus

Dench had passed the last hours of his life . . .

He went over to the broad stone porch, mounted the shallow steps, and tried the big door. It was fastened. He had expected little else. If anyone, for reasons of their own, had been using this house, which the state of the chain on the gate seemed to indicate, they would probably have affected an entrance at the back.

Forcing his way through the mass of briars and tangled undergrowth which grew in wild profusion close up to the house, he made his way to the rear of the premises. He came upon a scattered group of outbuildings and the paved yard that lay in front of the garage. There should, if his memory was not playing him false, be a door somewhere near, a door giving admittance to the scullery. He found it, laid his hand on the handle, and — it opened! Somebody *had* been using the place. He paused, peering into the blackness of the interior. A musty smell came to his nostrils, the smell of a house long shut up.

Stepping across the threshold, he

listened with straining ears for the slightest sound which might warn him that others besides himself were near at hand. But no sound reached him. Taking his torch from his pocket, he sent a broad fan of light cutting through the darkness. It revealed a big scullery. A copper loomed in one corner and a huge sink with tarnished taps, full of dust and grime.

Through an open door facing him he caught a glimpse of the kitchen: a dresser full of crockery, a table, chairs, and a linoleum-covered floor, thick with the accumulated dust of those three intervening years. And in the dust were marks, the marks of recent footprints!

He closed the door and moved forward, carefully avoiding those tell-tale smudges. Huge cobwebs, the relics of dynasties of spiders, draped everything with filmy grey curtains. The range, rusty and heaped with rubbish, yawned blackly, and in the midst of all this neglect — a striking contrast — stood a cheap tin candlestick which was brand new. It stood on the table, and contained three quarters of a candle that had guttered badly. Footprints, too, were all over the place: clear evidence, with the candle, the open door, and the severed chain, that this derelict mansion had received visitors.

Mr. Budd crossed over to the candlestick, and was in the act of picking it up when he heard a sound. It came from somewhere in the front of the house, the opening and closing of a door!

He switched out his torch and stood in the dark, tense and alert. Voices reached his ears: the deep, muffled tones of a man, followed, to his surprise, by the softer, unmistakable voice of a woman.

Stealthily he crept forward. The kitchen door was ajar, and he pulled it open, staring along the dark passage which emerged into the big hall. He saw a glimmer of light and a distorted shadow sprawled over the wall of the passage.

'The light should be still on,' said the woman's voice. 'The switch is just by the door.'

'I've found it.' The man's answer culminated in a click and the hall became lit with the soft radiance of a shaded electric bulb. 'Mind how you go. Everything's thick with dust.'

'Nobody's been here for three years,' answered the woman. 'Not since — not since Father died.'

Mr. Budd's pent-up breath expelled itself slowly through his parted lips. 'Is that Miss Marsh?' he called, and was answered by a stifled scream.

'Who's that?' demanded the man harshly, and the superintendent moved forward and emerged into the wide, dust-sheeted hall. 'I'm sorry if I startled you, miss,' he apologised. 'Perhaps you remember me. Superintendent Budd, of Scotland Yard.'

The two people who stood by the main entrance stared at him as though he were a ghost. The woman was tall and slim, a slimness which, in some curious way, was enhanced by the fur coat she wore, and she was very lovely. There are some women who strike one as beautiful at first glance but whose beauty fades upon analysis. There are others, a rare type, whose loveliness only grows on one at each succeeding meeting, and fewer still

35

whom one can catalogue as beautiful at first sight and never find cause afterwards to change that first opinion.

Cathleen Marsh came into this last category. She was young, between twenty-three and twenty-four, and her wide-set eyes under long lashes were of that uncommon colour which is neither blue nor violet but a mixture of the two. In no single feature was her face perfect, but the combination formed a completely satisfying picture with which no fault could be found.

'I — I remember you,' she said huskily, her face pale. 'What are you doing here?'

'I'm afraid I gave you a bit of a shock, miss,' said Mr. Budd. 'But you gave me one, too, so it's mutual.'

'Weren't you the detective who was in charge of the Marsh case?' inquired the man, frowning.

'Yes, that's right, sir,' said Mr. Budd, stifling a yawn. 'You're Mr. Rutherford, aren't you?'

'That's right,' said the other, nodding. 'I remember you now, Superintendent.'

'But — but I don't understand,' said

the woman, her eyes wide. 'What are you doing here? How did you get in?'

'The door at the back was open, miss,' explained Mr. Budd, 'and I came to have a look round. Somebody seems to have been usin' this place without authority.'

'Somebody using it?' Rutherford's tone was sharp. 'Who?'

'I can't tell you that,' said the big man, shaking his head.

'But I still don't understand.' Cathleen Marsh's voice was puzzled. 'Why — how — What brought you here?'

'Well, miss,' said Mr. Budd, 'it 'ud take a lot of explainin'. But I'm workin' on that business — I daresay you've read about it — the Dench murder. And somethin' I discovered led me to suppose that maybe I should find a clue here.'

'A clue here — to the Dench murder?' said Rutherford incredulously. 'That's the man who disappeared and was found in a tunnel or something, isn't it?'

'That's right, sir,' said Mr. Budd. 'And I'm rather under the impression that between the time of his disappearance and the time he was found in the tunnel he was kept a prisoner — here!'

'Good God!' The other was startled. 'What makes you think that?'

Mr. Budd explained, and they listened interestedly. 'I suppose it could have been possible,' muttered Rutherford. 'The house was empty and nobody in the neighbourhood would be likely to come here, not after what happened.'

'That's what I was thinkin',' said the superintendent. He looked curiously from the tall, dark man to the woman. 'What brought you here?' he asked.

'Surely Miss Marsh has a right to come to her own house — ' began Rutherford, but the woman interrupted him.

'I came,' she said, 'because I'm thinking of reopening the place.'

Mr. Budd raised his eyebrows. 'You mean you're goin' to live here again, miss?' he asked.

She gave a little shiver. 'No, no!' she answered hastily. 'I could never live here again after what happened. But I'm going to open it temporarily.'

'If you take my advice, Miss Marsh,' said Rutherford, 'you'll give up this crazy idea. I don't see what possible good can come of it.'

Her mouth set obstinately. 'Perhaps you don't, Mr. Rutherford,' she answered coolly. 'But I've no intention of giving it up, all the same. I intend to find out who was responsible for the death of my father.'

Rutherford shrugged his shoulders. 'Well, I've advised you,' he said curtly, 'and I can do no more.'

Mr. Budd was curious. 'How d'you intend, miss,' he inquired, 'to go about findin' your father's murderer? It's three years now since the crime was committed, and although Scotland Yard are still workin' on it nothin's been discovered.'

'I know,' she answered quietly. 'Perhaps I shall be more fortunate. Since my father's death this place has been closed; I have been living with my aunt at the house in London. But for a long time I've had in my mind the idea which I now intend to carry out.' She paused and fingered her bag nervously. 'I'm going to reopen this house,' she went on, 'and I'm going to invite a party of friends for the weekend, the same people who were here three years ago. Among those people is the person who killed my father.'

Mr. Budd pursed his lips and gently scratched his chin. 'I don't know what good you think it'll do, miss,' he said dubiously. 'D'you imagine for a moment that the murderer is likely to give himself away after all this lapse of time?'

'I don't know,' she said in a low voice. 'I'm just hoping that something will happen to show us who — who it was.'

'Ever since Miss Marsh first mentioned her idea to me I've tried my best to dissuade her,' said Rutherford.

'I've already made arrangements for the house to be cleaned, and issued some of the invitations,' said the woman stubbornly. 'And I'm determined. You needn't come unless you like, Mr. Rutherford — '

'Of course I shall come!' said Rutherford. 'But as your lawyer I have a certain duty to perform. Having done that — advised you against the whole thing — there's nothing more to be said.'

'When d'you intend to have this party?'

inquired Mr. Budd sleepily.

'The week after next,' said the woman. 'That will be the third of October. It will take nearly a fortnight to get the house ready, by the look of it. I suppose,' she added as a thought struck her, 'I suppose, Superintendent, you couldn't come, too?'

Mr. Budd considered. The woman's idea both interested and puzzled him. He wondered why, after a lapse of three years, she had suddenly decided on this plan. It was queer; queerer, too, coming immediately on the top of the murder of Dench, always supposing that there was a connection between the two crimes.

'I should have to get permission from the Yard,' he said after a pause. 'Not that I suppose that 'ud be very difficult. 'What I *don't* see is how anythin' can come of this idea of yours, miss.'

'Supposing nothing does come of it?' she said. 'It can't do any harm to try. *I* want to know who killed my father, and why he was killed. I *must* know, and your presence may help. Please come if you can.'

'If I can I will,' said the stout man, and

never dreamed into what a maze of horror and mystery the promise was to lead him.

'Now, if you don't mind,' he went on, 'I'll have a look round at the back and see if I can find any traces that might identify these people who've been usin' your house.'

'What makes you think this man — what's his name, Dench — should have been brought here?' asked the lawyer.

'Just a hunch,' said Mr. Budd. 'Nothin more. But I found a scrap of paper in an old suit of his with this address.'

'Dench? Dench?' the woman muttered, frowning. 'I don't remember the name.'

'Maybe I'm wrong,' said the superintendent. 'Maybe the people who've been here were just tramps. Still, I'd like to make sure, all the same.'

He went back into the kitchen, found the switch, and put on the light. The marks on the floor showed conclusively that more than one person had been there, but he found no other traces. It had occurred to him that possibly this had been the place where Dench had met his death, but there was no sign of blood.

Rutherford joined him just as he was finishing, a frown on his dark, good-looking face. 'I don't like this idea of Miss Marsh's at all,' he said. 'But she's set on it, and there you are.'

'I don't see that it can do any harm,' remarked Mr. Budd slowly. 'And I don't see that it can do any good. What's she hopin' to gain?'

'God knows!' said the lawyer with a gesture. 'If any of these people were responsible for that murder three years ago they're not likely to give themselves away. I should think it was more than probable they wouldn't come.'

Mr. Budd thought so, too, but they were both wrong. Every one of those people who had been present at the time Hebert Marsh came by his tragic death accepted the invitation sent them, and assembled in that ill-fated house where death had come once and, did they but know it, was to come again, stalking through the gloomy rooms and corridors with terror in its train.

3

The House-Party

During the ensuing days Mr. Budd made
no headway into his investigations concerning the death of James Augustus
Dench. In spite of all his inquiries he
found himself up against a dead end. The
man had been respectable, and no
amount of probing into his past could
bring to light any motive for his death.
The firm of safe-makers for whom he had
worked gave him an excellent character,
and there was nothing at all to account
for his mysterious disappearance and
subsequent murder.

Mr. Budd had an interview with the
assistant-commissioner, and explained his
difficulties. Colonel Blair listened without
comment till he had finished. 'So you're
under the impression,' he said, tapping
his fingers thoughtfully on his blotting
pad, 'that Dench's murder is connected

with the Hebert Marsh crime?'

'I've got an idea it is, sir,' said the big man. 'But I've nothin' very much to back it up.'

The colonel looked at him quizzically. 'You've had hunches like that before, haven't you, Superintendent?' he remarked. 'And in nine cases out of ten they've turned out right. Well, if you want to join this house party on October the third, go to it.'

'I'm not expectin' anythin' to come of it,' said Mr. Budd, 'but I'd like to be there. It's interestin' and peculiar that this woman should suddenly take it into her head to invite all these people to the house again. There's somethin' behind it, and I'd very much like to know what.'

'I'm inclined to agree with you,' said the assistant-commissioner. 'Let's hope you'll kill two birds with one stone, Budd. Find the murderer of Marsh and also solve the Dench business.'

'That 'ud be somethin' of a miracle, sir,' said the detective, and Colonel Blair shrugged his shoulders. 'Miracles sometimes happen,' he answered, 'even in these enlightened days.'

'Never when you want 'em to, sir,' said Mr. Budd, shaking his head. 'And that 'ud be the most unlikely miracle of all.'

He went back to his office, wrote a short note to Cathleen Marsh informing her that he would be pleased to accept her invitation, and pressed a button for a messenger. When the man came in answer to his ring he gave an order, and slumped back in his chair, his mind going back over the years.

Those people at Wildcroft Manor, when Hebert Marsh had been killed, had been a queer crew. He'd been convinced at the time that one of them had been responsible for the crime, but although countless inquiries had been made and they'd all been kept under observation, no evidence had been discovered to warrant an arrest.

Marsh himself had been a funny fellow, too. Plenty of money there, rich as blazes, but where it came from nobody seemed to know. He had had an office in the city, and was supposed to be a broker, but the profits from the deals he did wouldn't have kept a fly alive; and yet he'd had a fine house in town and that big place at Kings Mailing — and a bank balance that ran into five figures. There'd been some crooked stuff somewhere, but no amount of patient inquiry had unearthed it. His sister, too, that unpleasant old woman — she'd had money at one time; a fortune that was left her by an uncle who had died abroad. But every penny of that had gone — somewhere. When her brother died she hadn't a cent. He'd left all his money to his daughter, and the old woman was entirely dependent on her niece for everything.

His thoughts were interrupted by the return of the messenger with a bulky folder which he laid on the desk and then silently withdrew. Mr. Budd hoisted himself to a sitting posture and flipped it open with a thumb, refreshing his memory with the contents. He found a list of the people who had been involved, and studied it. There was the old woman, Emily Marsh, a queer old girl not quite all there. George Devine, the author, and his wife Alice. John Krayle, a friend of

Marsh's and a man of independent means. Gerald Trainor, who had no business, either. And Leslie Curtis, foppish, over-dressed. He remembered them all. A funny crowd. A queer crowd. And Pullman, the butler, an old man whose head was bald and with a lined, yellow face and a mouth that drooped at the corners. Queer was right. And now once again, if Cathleen Marsh's plan came off, all these people would be gathered together in the old house as they had been three years ago.

The big man closed the folder and lay back in his chair with closed eyes. It would be interesting to see how they reacted when they met again in surroundings that for all of them must be still pregnant with tragedy.

★   ★   ★

The weather changed during the next few days. The frost gave place to rain, and on that Saturday evening when Mr. Budd set off in his dingy car for Kings Mailing it was wild and stormy. The melancholy

Leek, huddled in an overcoat, sat silently beside him. He had decided to take the sergeant, although he was not included in the invitation. He could put up in the village and be on hand if he was wanted. Not that Mr. Budd imagined that he would be.

Cathleen Marsh's scheme was wild and impracticable. Did she think that the guilty person's nerve would break? It had held good for three years; had held good in face of all the questions and stringent inquiries at the time, and it was not likely the atmosphere of the old house and a reconstruction of the setting of the crime would shake it.

And yet — such cases had been known. In spite of his scepticism, the big man felt an inward excitement, a feeling of expectancy, as each turn of the wheels brought him nearer to his destination. He dropped Leek at the station sergeant's cottage, ran his car into a garage, and continued the rest of the way on foot. As he came up the dark avenue of poplars he saw lights glimmering in the windows of the manor house.

He was admitted to the big hall, swept now and dusted, and warmly lit, by Pullman, unchanged since he had last seen him three years ago. The old butler took his bag and set it down by the big staircase. 'Miss Marsh hasn't allotted the rooms yet, sir,' he said in his thin, quavering voice, and at that moment Cathleen Marsh came out of a door on the left.

'I'm so glad you were able to come,' she said with a smile. 'Pullman will take your hat and coat.'

Mr. Budd shed the garment and looked round approvingly. 'You've made it very comfortable here, miss,' he murmured. 'Nobody 'ud think it had been shut up all that time.'

'It involved a lot of work,' said the woman. 'Come into the lounge. You know everybody, I think.'

She led the way into the room from which she had emerged. The little hum of voices that had been going on ceased as they entered, and the big man became conscious that every eye was fastened on him. Sleepily he surveyed the group, and it might have been only yesterday since he had seen them before.

Lionel Hope, small and round, with a little dark moustache and large, horn-rimmed glasses that gave him the appearance of an owl, had altered not at all.

George Devine, tall, thin, with a thatch of jet-black hair that badly needed cutting, and arms that were so long that they almost reached to his knees, still wore the perpetual sneer which Mr. Budd remembered so well. Not a very pleasant personality. Nor his wife, Alice, a stout woman with very black eyes and skin the colour of putty, unhealthy-looking and slightly blotchy.

John Krayle, slight and pale, and Gerald Trainor, broad-faced, sturdy. Leslie Curtis, with the lazy grey eyes and the graceful carriage.

They hadn't changed one atom. Nor had the woman seated in the chair in the shadow by the great fireplace. Emily Marsh's emaciated face, with the sunken eyes and dry, brittle-looking grey hair, was just the same as she had been three years ago.

'You must be very cold after your

journey,' said Cathleen. 'Go and get warm by the fire while I fix up the rooms.'

She went away, calling to Pullman, and Mr. Budd moved over to the fire. His entrance had effectually stopped all conversation. The people in the room were watching him covertly, and on every face there was a look of fear and uneasiness.

The woman came back after a short delay. 'I'll tell you which rooms you're having now,' she said, 'and then you can go and tidy yourselves for dinner. Don't trouble to dress. We're going to be quite informal.'

The shrill voice of Alice Devine answered her. 'Can I have the room at the end of the corridor?' she said. 'The one I had — ' She stopped awkwardly, blushed, and stammered.

'I've given it to you,' said Cathleen calmly. 'You're all having the same rooms as you had before.'

'There are two extra people.' The thin voice of the old woman came from the fireplace. 'Where are you going to put them?'

'One of them will have to have Father's room,' said the woman.

'Surely — surely,' whispered Alice Devine, 'you're not — not going to ask anyone to sleep — *there*!'

'There are ten of us and ten rooms,' Cathleen said. 'Somebody must have it.'

'I'll have it,' said John Krayle. 'I'm not superstitious.' He lit a cigarette.

'Very well,' said the woman quietly. 'I was going to give it to Mr. Rutherford, but as he hasn't arrived yet it will make no difference.'

Pullman had come silently in, and the stout man saw that his face had gone a sickly green. The man was in a paroxysm of fear. The room that had been allotted to him was on the top floor, and he went up to wash and unpack. It was quite a comfortable apartment, but there were evidences of hasty cleaning. The dust of three years had not been easy to remove in so short a time.

Rutherford had arrived when he came down, and shortly after, dinner was served. It was a cheerless meal. Everybody seemed to be watching everyone else, and conversation came spasmodically, with long intervals of silence.

All their nerves are keyed up to breaking point, thought the watchful Mr. Budd, *and I'm not surprised. I wonder they came at all.*

He made one discovery which interested him. Three of the men there were in love with Cathleen Marsh. John Krayle could scarcely keep his eyes off the woman, and Gerald Trainor saw his interest and scowled darkly at his plate. Leslie Curtis was openly infatuated. *An interestin' situation*, thought the detective.

The meal dragged on. Outside, the wind had risen to a gale, and howled and shrieked round the house with an intermittent fury. There was a tension in the atmosphere, an unpleasant feeling that communicated itself to Mr. Budd, of expectancy. There was relief on the faces round him when Cathleen Marsh announced that coffee would be served in the lounge.

They went back to the big room, with its cushioned divans and rugs and blazing fire — a pleasant change from the gloom of the panelled dining room. Rutherford came over to his side while the others were fixing a bridge table.

'Well, what do you think of it?' asked the lawyer under his breath. 'This — this horrible idea of Cathleen Marsh's?'

'Well, candidly, I don't like it, sir,' said the superintendent.

'Neither do I!' declared Rutherford. 'Look at them, pretending to behave normally and all scared to death.'

'Of what?' muttered Mr. Budd.

'Yes — of what?' the lawyer repeated. 'I'm glad you're here, Superintendent. Very glad indeed.'

And, surprisingly, Mr. Budd felt a shiver run down his spine, and the hair on the back of his neck prickled.

* * *

That first evening at Wildcroft Manor was destined to live long afterwards in the superintendent's memory. Pullman came in and removed the coffee cups, and although the terror which Mr. Budd had seen in his yellow face previously was no longer there, the old man's hands were shaking and he exhibited every sign of uneasiness and fear. Neither was he the only one.

On the faces of all that queer collection of people was a look of troubled anxiety; and, although they attempted a pretence of normality, they were stiff and constrained, both in their movements and conversation. There was an atmosphere of expectancy and gloom that hung like a pall over the whole house. The gaunt old woman had gone straight back to her corner by the big fireplace and sat hunched up in her chair, staring motionless into the flames. The big man, ensconced in one corner of a settee that was in partial shadow, smoked and watched. Outside, the night was noisy. The rush of the wind came in blustering gusts, blowing the rain violently against the window panes and shaking the trees until they creaked and groaned in protest.

Inside, in spite of the cosiness of the room and the warmth of the blazing fire, there seemed to the detective to be forces equally as violent; emotions that were being suppressed. He was not given to fancies, and yet there might have been an unseen person present — the dead owner of this great rambling mansion looking on ironically, and waiting for the breaking of strained nerves . . .

Mr. Budd, his eyes half-closed, the smouldering cigar between his fingers, examined each of the people in that room dispassionately. Who among them was responsible for the death of Hebert Marsh, and what motive had prompted the crime? Was the murderer one of those four playing bridge at the table under the standard lamp? The pale-faced Krayle? The thin, black-haired Devine? His stout, unhealthy-looking wife? Or the lazy-eyed Curtis? Or was it none of these? Perhaps it was the stout, bespectacled Lionel Hope, seated in an easy chair and desultorily turning the pages of an American magazine, with his eyes moving restlessly all the time as he kept a vigilant watch under cover of his pretence of reading. Or maybe Gerald Trainor, talking in low tones to Cathleen and Rutherford.

It was as difficult to tell now, as it had

been three years ago when the superintendent had exhausted every means in his power to discover the truth. More difficult, for time must have erected a guard against self-betrayal and brought with it a sense of security. There was little likelihood, he thought, of Cathleen Marsh's experiment proving successful.

The guilty person had kept the secret for three years and was not likely to yield it up under these somewhat theatrical conditions. And yet if there was a connection between the murder of Hebert Marsh and James Augustus Dench, as he believed, something had occurred to disturb the security of the killer. For if the same hand which had driven that knife into the back of the harmless and insignificant Dench had also sent the fatal bullet crashing through the brain of Hebert Marsh, the two crimes must be linked by a common motive. Was the recent killing part of the scheme which had included the previous one, or had it only been rendered necessary in the light of later events? The latter supposition seemed the most probable. If it was closely connected with Marsh's death, why wait three years? Or was this period of inactivity on the murderer's part essential to the plan, whatever it was?

'I'm not going to play any longer!' Mrs. Devine threw down her cards suddenly and rose to her feet. 'I hate this place!'

'Oh, come!' Krayle muttered. 'We must finish the rubber.'

'I'm not going to play anymore!' declared the woman. 'Get somebody else to take my place.' She moved over to the fire and warmed her hands.

Devine looked round. 'Anyone like to take my wife's place?' he asked.

'I will if you like,' said Rutherford reluctantly, and approached the table. As he sat down in the chair which the woman had vacated there came three soft taps on the window pane.

'What was that?' cried Alice Devine shrilly, and her eyes had gone wide with terror.

They listened, rigid figures, as though they had all been suddenly turned to stone. For a moment there was only the wild tumult of the wind, the sighing of the trees; and then once again came a gentle tapping at the window.

Krayle's face went livid and he half-rose, gripping the arms of his chair. 'What in God's name — ' he said.

'It's nothin' to be alarmed about,' said Mr. Budd gently. He had hauled himself to his feet and was peering out into the night. 'The creeper or somethin' has broken loose and the wind's bangin' it against the window.'

'Oh, is that all?' Krayle breathed the words in relief, and the colour came slowly back to Alice Devine's pasty face. 'I thought — it sounded like — like fingers . . . '

The bridge players settled down to the game, but the incident had left its mark. The undercurrent of fear which had been present all the time was now clearly visible on the surface.

Mr. Budd had a curious feeling that there was a crisis approaching. It came to him suddenly, that sixth sense that had never let him down. There was tragedy in the air.

That interminable evening was brought to an end by Emily Marsh. At half-past ten she got suddenly to her feet and harshly announced that she was going to bed.

'I think we're all fairly tired,' said Cathleen, and there was a chorus of agreement.

Everybody seemed anxious to seek the seclusion of their own rooms and the opportunity it offered to drop the mask with which each was endeavouring to conceal their feelings.

'Bolt your doors tonight!' said the old woman suddenly, pausing on the threshold, a gaunt figure that was queerly menacing. 'Bolt your doors and your windows, too! This is an evil house!'

They stared at her, white-faced, and a curious little sobbing cry escaped the lips of Alice Devine. 'Don't!' she muttered brokenly. 'Don't!'

'Hebert died here, shot in the night!' cried Emily Marsh. 'And until now the place has been closed. Perhaps death will come again, as it did three years ago!' She swung round without another word, went out, and slammed the door behind her.

For nearly a minute after she had gone the people in the room remained motionless. Mr. Budd, scanning the faces before him, saw that they one and all depicted fear — in some cases sheer terror. What had the old woman meant by her words? Did she know something? If so she must know, or at least suspect, the identity of the murderer . . .

The big man was so busily occupied with his own thoughts that it was only mechanically that he answered the vague good-nights that were flung at him as that strange assembly began to break up.

He sought his own room and closed the door, sighing with relief at finding himself alone. The strain of the evening had made him feel physically tired, but his brain was alert and wakeful. Sitting on the edge of the bed, he lit a cigar and ran over in his mind the events of that queer evening. There had been nothing in the behaviour of any one particular person to give rise to suspicion. They were all strung up — all with nerves on edge, but that was scarcely to be wondered at. Stolid, phlegmatic, as he was himself, he had reacted unpleasantly to that atmosphere of tension and fear. Why were they all afraid? It was understandable that one among them should be, but not all.

He finished his cigar, crushed out the glowing butt in an ashtray on the bedside table, and yawning, rose to his feet and began leisurely to remove his jacket.

Outside the wind was still blowing strongly, although the rain had ceased. Going over to the window, he peered out. A bleary moon shone fitfully, and across the sky banks of angry clouds, their edges ragged and wind-torn, were scudding. A wild night, full of strange noises, which found echoes in the old house. An appropriate setting for tragedy — stark, bare tragedy, such as three years ago had been enacted here.

Mr. Budd drew the curtains, and as he did so, without warning, a loud report drowned the minor sounds of the storm; an explosion that seemed to shake the house. It came like a thunderbolt from somewhere below, and was followed immediately by the heavy sound of a fall.

Mr. Budd was at the door with surprising celerity, and had wrenched it open almost before the echoes of the shot had died. A dim light on the stairway threw uncertain shadows as he hurried along the corridor and down the stairs to the floor below.

Voices came to him — excited, alarmed voices — and he saw Gerald Trainor, fully dressed, peering out of the open door of his bedroom. The man saw him at the same moment.

'What was it? What was it?' he demanded.

'I'm just goin' to see,' answered the big man.

'It was a shot I think. It came from the floor below,' muttered Trainor. 'My God! What can have happened?'

But Mr. Budd had no time to answer him. He, too, was desperately anxious to discover the meaning of that report, and when he reached the next landing he found it.

The door of John Krayle's room, the room in which Marsh had died, was open and a light streamed forth. It came from the lamp over the bed, and peering in, the stout man saw Krayle lying on his face on the floor — an inert, sprawling figure in purple striped pyjamas. His feet were bare, and from under his body oozed a dark trickle of blood.

With a quick intake of his breath the detective entered the room, bent down, and turned the motionless figure over. John Krayle had been shot. The breast of his pyjama jacket was wet with blood, and on the left side of his chest was a tiny reddish-blue hole almost immediately above the heart!

4

The Poem

The whole thing was horrible. Here was a repetition of what had occurred three years before, an almost exact duplicate of the murder of Hebert Marsh.

Seasoned to ugliness in all its forms as he was, Mr. Budd could not repress a feeling of nausea as he gazed down at the dead man, but he pulled himself together and motioned Trainor, who was about to stoop over the body, to stand back.

'Don't touch anything!' he snapped. 'And don't tread about the room, please!'

Trainor, white-faced and startled, obeyed. Doors were opening and shutting, and the sound of shuffling feet and excited voices reached their ears. Devine appeared in the open doorway, his tall, lean form wrapped in a bathrobe, his long face white and scared.

'What is it?' he demanded shakily.

'What's happened?'

'Mr. Krayle has been shot!' replied Mr. Budd shortly; and, as the other made a movement forward, 'No, don't come in, please. I don't want anybody to come further than the door.'

Alice Devine, her face shining with cold cream, her eyes wide with terror, peered over her husband's shoulder. 'Shot!' she wailed. 'Oh, my God! Just like Hebert!'

'Shut up!' growled her husband angrily.

'What's happened?' It was Leslie Curtis, pushing the crowd at the door aside, and then as he saw that still figure on the floor: 'Great Heaven!'

'Don't come any further than the door!' repeated Mr. Budd. 'Nothing in this room must be touched until the police have seen it.'

'The police!' came a croaking voice. 'What good are the police? What good did they do before?' A queer figure in a dressing gown, Emily Marsh forced herself to the front of the frightened group. 'I told you all to lock your doors. He was a fool not to heed my warning!'

'Aunt Emily!' Calm, tall and white-faced,

Cathleen came to her aunt's side and took her arm. 'Come away — come back to your room.'

The old woman opened her thin lips, closed them with a snap, and allowed herself to be led away.

Mr. Budd looked around him. Krayle had evidently not gone to bed — the clothes were undisturbed. On the table by the bedside was a book and his horn-rimmed glasses. The glasses were powerful ones; without them he must have been almost blind.

Near the foot of the bed lay an extraordinary object — at least extraordinary to find in the bedroom of a private house. It was a fireman's helmet, rather old and tarnished. There was a large dent in one side of it, and the nail on which it had evidently been hung was still fixed in the brass-work of the chinstrap.

Mr. Budd looked at it curiously, picked it up and turned it over and over in his hands. 'Does anybody know who this belongs to?' he murmured.

'Marsh, I suppose,' said Trainor.

The fat man looked inside. There was

an inscription roughly scratched on the metal. '*Property of John Crillum. Garvand Street Fire Station. W. C.*'

'Doesn't appear to have been his,' he murmured, and frowned.

Cathleen Marsh came back at that moment and stood in the doorway, looking from the figure on the floor to the stout man. 'Is — is he — dead?' she whispered. Mr. Budd nodded.

'Yes, miss,' he answered. 'I'm afraid he is.'

'Who did it?' she asked huskily.

'I don't know,' he said, shaking his head. 'Somebody in this house.'

'But that's all nonsense!' broke in George Devine brusquely. 'Who could have wanted to kill Krayle?'

'I'm not suggestin' a motive!' retorted Mr. Budd coldly. 'I'm merely statin' a fact. The man has been shot, and somebody in the house shot him!'

An uneasy silence followed his words.

'Nobody must leave until the local police have been notified,' the detective went on. 'Perhaps you wouldn't mind ringin' up the station, Miss, and tellin'

Inspector Tipman what's happened. He'll know what to do.'

'The phone isn't connected,' said Cathleen in a low voice.

Mr. Budd pursed his lips and scratched his chin. 'That's rather awkward,' he remarked. 'Maybe your man, Pullman, 'ud take a message.'

'I'll go if you like,' said Gerald Trainor.

'Thank you, sir,' said Mr. Budd, 'but I'd rather no one left the house, if you don't mind. You'll oblige me if you'll all go down to the lounge. I'll want a word with you presently.'

There was a grumbling murmur from the group.

'I'll see if I can find Pullman,' said Cathleen, and at that moment the yellow-faced butler put in an appearance, sketchily attired in a coat over his pyjamas and accompanied by a woman, stout and red-faced, whom Mr. Budd recognised as the cook, Mary Hutton.

'Mr. Krayle has been killed,' said the woman. 'Mr. Budd wants you to take a message to the police station, Pullman. Will you dress at once?'

The butler, his face ghastly, his staring eyes fixed in a horrified fascination on the sprawling figure by the bed, nodded. 'Yes, miss,' he answered almost inaudibly.

'Make up the fire in the lounge, too,' said Mr. Budd, and with another nod the old man moved away.

Whispering among themselves, the others departed reluctantly, and left to himself the superintendent made a quick search of the room. The window was fastened and snibbed on the inside. The murderer must have come and gone by the door.

There was no sign of a weapon, which precluded any possibility of suicide, even if Mr. Budd had entertained such an idea for a moment, which he did not. This was very obviously murder. The loudness of the shot suggested that it had been fired from the passage through the open door of Krayle's room.

Idly he picked up the book which the dead man had apparently been reading. It was an old volume by Anthony Trollope, and he was about to put it down again when he saw something scrawled in pencil on the fly-leaf. It was a short verse and he read it with drawn brows.

'Midnight and the air is foul
With flying figures rushing fast
Toward the wood. A ghostly band,
   they howl
And shriek with frenzied glee as they
   go past
Into the night to meet Asmodeus.
A dreadful chorus, with a wailing croon,
Across the fair face of the Witches'
   Moon!'

It conveyed nothing to Mr. Budd, and with a grunt he closed the book and put it back where he had found it. There was nothing else of interest in the room, and removing the key from the inside he went out, closed the door and locked it, putting the key in his pocket.

Going down to the hall he met Pullman, dressed and evidently about to set forth on his journey to the police station. Before he left, the superintendent made him go a round of the house, examining the doors and windows. They were all locked and bolted. He put a question to the trembling old man.

'No, sir,' replied the butler. 'I haven't touched them. I went round and saw that they were all fastened before going to bed and I haven't touched them since.'

'You're willing to swear that?' said Mr. Budd.

'I'm willing to swear that, sir,' answered Pullman.

Mary Hutton, the cook, made the same statement. She had not been near any of the doors or windows. She'd gone to bed directly after she had washed up the dinner things, and had slept until the sound of the shot had wakened her.

The detective completed his round of the house, saw Pullman depart for Mallington, and when he entered the lounge there was no doubt in his mind. The killer had *not* come from without.

He surveyed the drawn faces of the people by the fire, and when he spoke his voice was grave. 'The person who shot Mr. Krayle didn't come from outside,' he said, watching them keenly. 'And there's no one concealed in the house. The doors and windows are all closed and tightly fastened. Even if it had been possible for anyone to have got in, they couldn't have got away again after the alarm. That means the murderer is still here!'

Alice Devine made a little sighing sound as though she had been holding her breath for a long time, but no one else stirred.

'Now, I'm goin' to ask you,' went on Mr. Budd, after a pause, 'what you was all doin' when the sound of the report disturbed you. And I'll start with you, Mr. Trainor, if you don't mind. I found you at the door of your bedroom. How long had you been there?'

'Not more than a minute,' replied Trainor. 'I heard the shot and came to see what had happened.'

'You hadn't attempted to undress,' said the big man, 'although it was nearly two hours since you'd gone up to bed.'

'There's nothing in that!' protested Trainor. 'I wasn't feeling very tired. I sat smoking and listening to the wind.'

Mr. Budd made no comment on this explanation. 'When you came to your door,' he said, 'did you see anyone?'

'Only you,' Trainor answered. 'No one else.'

'Did you hear anythin' prior to the shot?' continued the stout man.

'No.' There was a faint hesitation in the reply.

'You're sure?' persisted Mr. Budd. 'You didn't hear anyone movin' about?'

'No,' said Trainor quickly.

'The shot, in my opinion,' went on Mr. Budd, 'was fired from the corridor.'

'From the corridor?' It was Leslie Curtis who spoke, and the superintendent nodded.

'Yes, I think so,' he said. 'That's why it was so loud.'

Nobody spoke for a moment, and then George Devine broke the silence. 'I thought it sounded very close,' he remarked.

'Oh, did you, sir?' Mr. Budd swung round to face him. 'How close?

'Almost outside my door,' replied the other.

'How long was it before you came out to see what had happened?' asked the detective.

'About a minute — it couldn't have been more,' said Devine.

'Was there anybody in the corridor?' queried the big man.

'Only my wife,' was the reply. 'She was just coming out of the door of her room.'

'Nobody else?' persisted Mr. Budd.

The other shook his shaggy head. 'Curtis came out of his room as you came down the stairs.'

Mr. Budd suppressed a yawn and rubbed his ample chin. Who had been in that corridor outside Krayle's room and fired the fatal shot? He questioned them all closely, but each swore that they had not left their rooms until the sound of the shot had disturbed them. Somebody was evidently lying, but who?

'Is anybody possessed of a pistol?' asked the stout man, and was answered by a concerted shaking of heads. 'I'm afraid I shall have to search all of you,' said Mr. Budd, 'and your rooms and belongin's.'

'Oh, come! That's going a bit too far — ' began Devine in protest.

The big man eyed him coldly. 'Have

you anythin' to conceal, Mr. Devine?' he inquired.

'No, of course not!' said the other violently. 'But dammit, nobody likes having their private property turned over by a stranger!'

'In this instance I'm afraid they'll have to put up with it,' murmured Mr. Budd. 'Murder is a serious business, sir, and likes and dislikes become of very little importance.' He turned to Leslie Curtis. 'I'll begin with you, if you don't mind, Mr. Curtis,' he said.

'I mind very much,' the young man drawled. 'But it doesn't seem any good minding. Go ahead!'

Mr. Budd ran his hands over him. He was wearing a dressing gown over his pyjamas and anything so bulky as a revolver or an automatic would have been instantly detectable. But there was nothing of the sort, nor did a search of the others yield anything in the nature of a weapon.

'I'll be obliged if you'll all wait here while I have a look through your various rooms,' said the superintendent, and left them grumbling to each other.

Ruling out Cathleen and himself, he made a diligent search of the bedrooms which had been occupied by the others, but he found nothing, and was not altogether surprised. The killer would have foreseen that a search was inevitable and got rid of the weapon at once. There were plenty of places where he could have hidden it in the first excitement following the shot.

One discovery he did make — a discovery that confirmed his idea of the place from which the shot had been fired. Lying close by the wall in the corridor, at a spot that was exactly opposite the door of Krayle's bedroom, he found a small brass cylinder — the ejected cartridge from an automatic pistol. The fumes of cordite still clung to it, and Mr. Budd slipped it into his pocket. When the doctor had made his examination and the bullet was extracted the two could be compared.

He went back to the lounge and waited in silence under the hostile eyes of the group by the fireplace for the coming of the police.

* * *

It was some time before Inspector Tipman arrived, and in the interval Mr. Budd held a consultation with Cathleen and Mark Rutherford. The woman was calm and composed, but clearly retaining her composure only by an effort. The death of Krayle had shocked and horrified her.

'It's all dreadful — terrible!' she whispered. 'I wish I'd never tried my plan.' She looked shockingly tired; her large eyes were dark with a haunting fear and she had deep purple shadows under them as though she hadn't slept for weeks.

'I advised you against it,' said the lawyer, 'although I never anticipated anything like this.'

'Neither did I,' she said. 'If I had — ' She left the sentence unfinished and shivered. 'Why — why do you think he was killed?' she asked.

'I've no idea, miss,' Mr. Budd said candidly. 'Any more than I've any idea why your father was killed. I'm only sure of one thing, and that is both murders were committed by the same person.'

They were speaking in a corner of the big lounge, watched by the group huddled round the fire.

'Nobody could have expected it,' muttered the woman. 'That such a thing should happen twice!' She was trying desperately to convince herself that she was not to blame.

'Of course no one could have expected it,' said the big man kindly. 'Don't you go worryin' yourself, miss. It wasn't your fault.'

Inspector Tipman, accompanied by a weary-eyed sergeant, a constable, and the divisional surgeon, put in an appearance just before three. Mr. Budd took him aside and explained the situation. The inspector listened without comment until he had finished, and then he uttered a low whistle.

'Queer business!' he muttered. 'The Marsh murder was before my time, but of course I've heard all about it. It's still discussed in the village. This seems to have taken place under practically the same conditions.'

'Almost exactly the same conditions,' agreed Mr. Budd,' except that durin' the Marsh crime there was a fog.'

'Not much doubt,' Tipman remarked, 'that one of the people in the house did it. The difficulty's going to be to find out which one.'

'It is,' said the detective with a weary yawn. 'And it's made more difficult because, with the exception of Miss Marsh, none of them want the truth to come to light.'

'But why don't they?' said the inspector. 'That's unnatural. You'd think they'd be only too glad, if only that they'd be cleared.'

'H'm! That's just the question,' murmured Mr. Budd thoughtfully. 'Would they?'

'What d'you mean?' asked the puzzled inspector.

'Would the truth clear 'em?' said the big man. 'Or would it in some way incriminate 'em all? It seems to me that there must have been some kind of shady work goin' on between 'em and Marsh.

I've always thought so. And now I'm more convinced than ever. They're all frightened of somethin', that's obvious, and it's my opinion that they're scared that somethin' they was doin' with Marsh may be discovered.'

'But what?' said Tipman.

'I haven't the least idea!' Mr. Budd murmured. 'But I'm pretty sure that's somewhere near the truth, and if we could find out what it was we should have the motive for Marsh's death and this other feller's.' He made no mention of his belief that the Dench crime was also connected. At the moment this was only a theory of his own. There would be time enough to talk to Tipman about it when he possessed more substantial evidence to go on.

'Well, we'd better get busy,' said the practical Tipman. He placed the constable on guard in the hall, called to the sergeant, and with Mr. Budd went upstairs to inspect the body. When he had examined it the divisional surgeon took his place, and after a brief interval made his report.

Krayle had apparently died instantly. The bullet had passed through the upper portion of the heart and made its exit beneath the left shoulder blade.

'Which means,' said Mr. Budd, 'it must be somewhere in the room. I didn't find it when I looked, but maybe we'll find it when we make another search.'

'I wonder what happened to the weapon?' said Tipman. 'If only we could find that — '

'We shan't!' broke in the superintendent. 'It's been too carefully concealed, you can bet your life on that!'

But he was wrong, for half an hour later the automatic was found — stuffed between the cushions of the settee in the lounge, and it was George Devine who found it.

He showed them where it was, and looked on while they examined the weapon. It was small — almost a toy — and made of blued metal. That it had fired the fatal shot there was no doubt. There was one cartridge missing from the clip, and the brass case which the stout man had picked up in the corridor fitted exactly.

'How did you come to find it?' he

asked, and Devine explained.

'Quite by accident,' he said. 'I was sitting fiddling about with the cushions when I touched something cold.'

'Have you ever seen this before?' asked Tipman, and was answered by a shake of the head.

'No, never!' declared the author.

Neither, apparently, had anyone else, though to one of them it must have belonged.

Another and more extensive examination was made of the bedroom. Krayle's clothing, which lay in an untidy heap on a chair at the foot of the bed, was searched, without finding anything of particular interest.

Mr. Budd had not examined the dead man's luggage previously, but now, with Tipman and the sergeant's help, he did so. Everything was packed carefully — Krayle had evidently been rather finicky — and at the bottom of the expensively fitted dressing case he made a discovery. Under a pile of handkerchiefs he found a little square green box. Opening it he looked in blank astonishment at the contents. Spare clips of cartridges!

Taking the brass shell from his pocket he compared it with the cartridges in the green box. They were identical. And there seemed only one explanation. Krayle had been shot with his own pistol.

'Queer!' said Tipman, rubbing the side of his red face. 'How did the murderer get possession of it?'

Mr. Budd could not tell him.

They completed their investigations in the room, lifted the body onto the bed, covered it with a sheet, and came out. While Tipman and the sergeant went to conduct a further questioning of the people in the lounge, Mr. Budd made his way out to the kitchen, where Mary Hutton and Pullman were sitting before the range. They got up as he entered, but he motioned them to be seated again, and leant against the edge of the table.

'I want to talk to you, Pullman,' he said. 'And you, too, Miss Hutton. You remember me, don't you?'

'Well enough,' muttered the woman.

'Three years ago,' said the stout man, 'your master was killed under similar circumstances to what happened tonight, and I put several questions to you then. You remember?'

The yellow-faced butler inclined his bald head, but the woman made no response. 'That's right, sir,' he said. 'But we didn't know anything about it, any more than we know about this. The first I knew anything was wrong was the noise of the shot — it woke me up.'

'And me, too,' said the woman quickly. 'We can't tell you much, mister.'

'You can tell me several things,' said Mr. Budd, eyeing them sleepily. 'You can tell me somethin' that I didn't ask you before. What sort of man was Mr. Marsh?'

'He was a very good master, sir,' said the butler quickly, and the cook nodded in confirmation.

'That's not an answer to my question,' persisted the big man. 'I said what sort of man was he?'

There was a pause.

'There was those who didn't like him,' said Pullman reluctantly.

'I see.' The superintendent looked at

him sharply. 'Who didn't like him?'

'Well, several people didn't,' said the butler vaguely.

'The people who were here spending the weekend with him? Didn't they like him?' asked Mr. Budd.

'Some pretended they did,' answered Pullman.

'Who pretended they did?' snapped the detective.

'Well . . . ' The old man was obviously ill at ease. 'Mr. Devine was one that you could see didn't. I caught him looking at the master several times when his back was turned and — well, it weren't a pretty look.'

'Anybody else?' prompted Mr. Budd.

'Miss Emily, sir. She never did get on with her brother. Always quarrelling, they was.'

'Why didn't you tell me this before?' demanded the superintendent.

'You didn't ask me, sir,' said the butler. 'And it wasn't my place to volunteer information.'

'It was your place,' said Mr. Budd severely, 'to tell anythin' you knew which was likely to help the police in their investigations.'

The old man was silent, and although the detective put several further questions concerning the character of Marsh, he succeeded in learning nothing more. He had certainly not been very popular, but then people are not as a rule killed because they are unpopular.

The day grew older, the hours passing with weary monotony. Inspector Tipman completed his preliminary investigations and retired, leaving the constable on guard in the hall. With daylight and properly donned clothing and Pullman coming and going, laying the table for breakfast, the nightmarish aspect of things had gone a little, but not much.

Nobody even pretended to eat anything. The empty chair which had been occupied on the previous night by John Krayle was a vivid reminder of the thing that lay awaiting the arrival of the ambulance behind the closed door upstairs.

Mr. Budd was the only one who did justice to Mary Hutton's cooking, and he made a normal breakfast.

The bullet had not been found; and after the meal, while he was waiting for the arrival of Leek, to whom he had dispatched a hurried note by Tipman, he decided to make another search. Wearily, for he was very tired, he mounted the stairs, and as he caught sight of the door of the bedroom where Krayle had met his death he drew in his breath sharply. He had left it shut and locked. Now it was open!

With quick strides he crossed the deserted corridor and peered in. The room, with the exception of the body on the bed, was empty. But somebody had been there. The book with the scrawled verse on the fly-leaf, which had been lying on the table by the side of the bed, had gone!

5

In the Night

Mr. Budd made a careful search in case it might have been knocked off the table. There was no sign of it anywhere. He felt in his pocket. The key of the room was there, where he had put it after locking the door.

He examined the door and discovered another key in the lock on the outside. Sometime during the morning someone had discovered a key that fitted, and taken the book. But why? Because of the verse scrawled on the flyleaf? It had conveyed nothing to the detective, and he had practically forgotten its existence.

He shrugged his shoulders. Whether it was because of the verse or for some other reason, the book had gone. Somebody had taken it. Who, and for what purpose? It had gone, and that was all there was to it.

He heard the sound of a door closing, and peering out into the passage saw Cathleen coming out of her aunt's room. He called to her softly and the woman came over to him. 'D'you mind coming in here for a moment or two, miss?' he said. 'I want to tell you something.' She hesitated for a second, and then, without a word, followed him into the room.

'What is it?' she asked in a low voice, keeping her eyes averted from the sheeted figure on the bed.

'Rather a queer thing has happened,' said Mr. Budd slowly. 'There was a book lyin' on that table,' he said, pointing, 'and it's gone. It was taken by someone durin' the mornin'.'

'Gone?' she whispered. 'But — but why?'

'I dunno,' Mr. Budd replied. 'But there must be some reason, and an urgent one, for its bein' taken.'

'What book was it?' Cathleen asked

'It was a story by a feller called Trollope,' said the superintendent. 'But it had a little verse scrawled in the front of it in pencil, somethin' about witches.'

She looked at him in amazement. 'It seems ridiculous!' she answered. 'Why should anybody want a book?'

'Well, somebody did,' said Mr. Budd. 'And they wanted it so badly that they took a big risk in gettin' it. Are all the locks the same on this floor, miss?'

'Yes,' she answered. 'I discovered that some years ago. Father locked the door of his room and lost the key, but we found that the next door key fitted.'

'So that accounts for the key,' murmured the fat man. He pursed his lips and his eyes strayed to the bed. 'What was Mr. Krayle's business?' he asked after a slight pause.

'I don't know,' she answered. 'I don't think he had any business.'

'Was he well off?'

'Oh, yes, quite — at least I think so.' She made the amendment quickly. 'I knew very little about him, really.'

'Your father and he were great friends, though, weren't they?' said Mr. Budd.

'They were together a lot,' she replied. 'I don't know whether they could be called great friends.'

'Miss Marsh,' said the big man, 'I'm goin' to ask you a question that may seem impertinent. And believe me I wouldn't ask it unless it was necessary. What kind of man was your father?'

Her eyes, which had been regarding him steadily, dropped. She twisted a fold of her dress between her fingers and her reply was so long in coming that he repeated his question.

'He — he was always very kind to me,' she whispered at last.

'That isn't what I asked,' said Mr. Budd gently.

'If you mean was he — liked by his friends, I can't tell you,' she said. 'I don't think so — you've seen some of them and the way they go on. You saw what they were like three years ago. You're better able to judge than I am.' She was keeping something back, of that he was certain.

'The only time's I've seen 'em,' said Mr. Budd thoughtfully, 'they've been scared. Surely they weren't always like that?'

'Yes, always,' she answered. 'But — but they hid it better. I believe,' she added

93

quickly, 'that they always hated Father — they accepted his hospitality but they hated him!'

He raised his eyebrows. 'That sounds queer to me,' he remarked. 'Why?'

'I don't know, but they did.' She paused and raised her eyes. 'They were glad when he was killed, all of them!'

'Includin' your aunt?' said Mr. Budd.

She started. 'Why do you say that?' she asked.

'Because I think she knows somethin' that she hasn't revealed,' said the superintendent. 'Somethin' that she's kept to herself, at the time your father was killed and for three years after. I should like to have a talk to her. If she could be persuaded to speak, I think maybe she could help us.'

'She's asleep now,' replied Cathleen doubtfully. 'When she wakes I'll take you to her.

'Thank you, miss.' He frowned and shook his head. 'There's somethin' very dark and sinister behind all this, and it's my opinion it's somethin' in your father's life that nobody knows anythin' about. If we could find the motive for his death it wouldn't be difficult to lay our hands on the murderer.'

She said nothing, and he changed the subject abruptly. 'Did you know that Mr. Krayle carried a pistol?' he asked, and she stared.

'A pistol?' she repeated. 'No. Did he?'

He took the automatic from his pocket and held it lightly in his hand. 'This was found in the cushions of the settee,' he said, 'and it belonged to Krayle. It was taken by the murderer and used to kill him.'

She looked at the little weapon fearfully and took it in her hand.

'Doesn't it strike you as peculiar, miss, that a man should come to a weekend party — armed?' said Mr. Budd softly.

'Do you mean — are you suggesting — ' she began.

'I'm suggestin', miss, that Mr. Krayle came armed because he knew he was in danger,' interrupted the big man. 'He expected an attempt on his life.'

The day was grey, and in the cold light the oval of her face looked paler than it really was. 'Then he knew — ' She left the sentence unfinished.

'The murderer,' he completed for her. 'Yes, miss, I think he did.'

'But — ' She stopped suddenly, turning her head towards the door. 'Excuse me,' she said. 'I think I heard my aunt calling.'

She hurried away, and Mr. Budd, who had heard nothing, was left wondering whether it had been an excuse or whether she had really imagined her aunt had called.

But she didn't come back, and shrugging his shoulders he began to carry out his search for the bullet. It was a long time before he eventually found it, and the reason why he had failed to do so before was evident. It was buried in the woodwork of the skirting under the window, close down near the floor, and practically invisible.

With his penknife he dug it out, peered at the little blob of metal, and slipped it into his pocket. Its position was peculiar. He glanced out into the corridor, drawing an imaginary line from the height of a normal person's hand to the spot where the bullet had lodged. It was a queer angle.

Krayle must have been crouching when the shot had struck him!

'Interestin' and peculiar,' murmured Mr. Budd, thoughtfully rubbing the back of his neck. For some time he stood motionless, staring sleepily at nothing in particular, and then he came out of the death room and closed the door.

A lean, shambling figure appeared at the end of the corridor and came towards him. 'I got your note and came along,' said Leek lugubriously. 'This is a funny business, ain't it?'

'It isn't making me laugh!' said Mr. Budd. 'Did Tipman tell you what had happened?'

'No, that sergeant feller, what's-'is-name, Wishit,' he answered. 'I didn't see Tipman. If you ask me it's a queer caper!'

'I don't ask you,' said the stout man. 'But you're about right. It is a queer caper. I can't get the hang of it at all. But there's a reason behind it, and I'm goin' to find it.'

'What I can't understand,' said the

sergeant, 'is why that woman suddenly took it into 'er 'ead to invite all them people 'ere. What made 'er so keen all of a sudden-like to find out who killed 'er father?'

'That's one of the things *I'd* like to know,' Mr. Budd replied slowly. 'For three years she makes no move, and then she suddenly wakes up. Yes, I'd very much like to know why.'

'Have you asked 'er?' suggested Leek brightly.

'No, I haven't asked her, and I'm not going to ask her!' said his superior irritably. 'I've got an idea she wouldn't tell me. This is a delicate business. There's all sorts of queer issues involved, in my opinion, and we've got to go careful.'

'What did you send for me for?' asked the sergeant.

'Well, the place seemed a bit gloomy,' said Mr. Budd, 'and I thought maybe your cheerful face 'ud brighten it up a bit. What d'you think I sent for you for? Did you imagine you was down here on holiday?'

'What I meant,' explained Leek patiently,

'was did you have any special job for me to do?'

The big man shook his head. 'No, not at the moment,' he answered. 'I just want you here in case of trouble.'

'Are you expectin' any more trouble?' inquired the sergeant.

'I'm not expectin' anythin'!' retorted Mr. Budd crossly. 'But I'm preparin' for all eventualities. Somewhere in this house there's a killer, and where there's a killer there's likely to be trouble, see?'

Leek saw only vaguely, but he nodded.

'Now come along down,' said Mr. Budd, 'and I'll introduce you to the menagerie. You've met 'em before, and they haven't changed much.'

They reached the hall just as a ring at the bell heralded the arrival of the ambulance. The body of John Krayle was carried downstairs and removed to the mortuary to await the inquest. For the rest of the day Inspector Tipman came and went, questioning, consulting with Mr. Budd, carrying out the thousand-and-one minor details which make up the routine investigation of a murder.

The night came down dark and silent, a contrast to the noisy boisterousness of the previous one. Sergeant Leek left just before dinner to return to his lodgings. The meal was a silent one, and afterwards nobody made any attempt to amuse themselves. No bridge table was brought out this evening. They sat morose and watchful, and made an early excuse to go to their rooms, either because they felt tired, or more likely on account of the fear which stalked among them.

At ten o'clock Mr. Budd found himself alone before the dying fire. Stooping to put on some more coal, he saw something lying near the copper scuttle. It was Krayle's book!

He picked it up and opened it. The flyleaf containing the verse was gone. It had been torn out!

'Queerer and queerer!' he muttered. 'Now what could anyone want with that?'

He made up the fire and sat for a long time, smoking and thinking, and it was nearly one when he rose stiffly, crossed the silent lounge, put out the light, and went upstairs to his room. He laid the book on the bedside table, undressed, and getting into bed fell almost instantly to sleep.

* * *

Mr. Budd found his torch, went to the door, and flashed the light out into the passage. It was deserted. Nothing stirred. The whole house was silent!

It was very cold, and he shivered slightly as he turned back into his room. One glance at the table near the bed-head and he saw the reason for the intruder's presence.

The book had gone!

His lips compressed. Why had it been taken a second time? Whoever had taken it in the first place had torn out the flyleaf, which was presumably what they wanted, and thrown the book away behind the coal scuttle. Why then had they taken all this trouble to get it back again? The big man scratched his head in bewilderment. It was a crazy jigsaw set by a madman. He started. Was that the explanation? Was the unknown insane? As a last resort he might have to come to that conclusion, but every other explanation would have to be tried first. The madman theory was too easy.

Slipping on a dressing gown, he went out into the corridor and silently and cautiously made his way down the stairs to the hall. The door of the lounge was open and he peered in. It was a vast place of echoing darkness which even the beam of the torch did little to dissipate. Long, ungainly shadows leaped and quivered on the walls, queer caricatures of the furniture, as he moved forward. But it was empty. Stopping in the middle of the room he listened, but there was no sound, nothing to indicate that another besides himself was wakeful.

He made his way to the kitchen quarters. Here the servants slept in two rooms opening onto a narrow passage. Both the doors were shut, and again there was no sound except a faint and unmusical snore.

As he turned to retrace his steps he saw a flicker of light come from the hall. Somebody was crossing it, carrying a candle. He made out a shadowy white figure, and then he saw who it was. Cathleen Marsh!

She gave a low cry as he approached, and in her terror almost dropped the candle.

'It's all right, miss. It's only me,' he whispered.

Her eyes were deep pools of fear, but there was relief in her voice when she spoke. 'You — you frightened me. What are you doing here?'

Briefly he explained.

'Who could it have been?' she said.

'I don't know,' he answered. 'I never had a chance to see, miss. What disturbed you?'

'I thought I heard somebody moving about,' she answered. 'Of course, it must have been you.' She pulled her wrap closer about her slim figure. 'It's all horrible! Horrible!' she whispered, and shivered.

'It's pretty puzzlin',' said Mr. Budd. 'I can understand why they wanted to take the book in the first place if that verse means anythin'. But why anyone should want to take it again is beyond me. I've been connected with some queer cases, but this beats them all! There are so many people who might be guilty.'

'And only one who is,' said the woman. 'What could that verse mean?'

He drew her into the warmer atmosphere of the lounge. 'I don't know,' he replied. 'But someone was very anxious to get it.'

'D'you think that's why they killed Mr. Krayle?' she whispered.

'No. It couldn't have been for that,' he answered. 'They didn't take it until afterwards.'

'I suppose — ' she began, and stopped.

'What?' he prompted gently.

'I was going to say, isn't it possible two murders can be separate — have no connection with one another?'

'I should say it was very unlikely,' he replied. 'It's too much of a coincidence, miss. Both shot, and under similar circumstances? No. There's a stamp about 'em that shows pretty clearly they were the work of the same hand. No,' he continued, 'if we solve one crime we shall solve the other.'

'I hope you're successful!' she said vehemently. 'It means a lot to me — more than you can imagine, to know for certain.' And then, abruptly: 'Oh, I've just thought of something. That verse. You said it was something to do with witches.'

'That's right, miss,' said Mr. Budd, a little astonished.

'Can you remember it?' she went on excitedly, laying her hand on his arm.

'No, I'm afraid I can't,' he said, shaking his head. 'I never was much good at poetry. It was somethin' about witches flyin' towards a wood across the moon. Lot of nonsense it sounded to me.'

'Across the moon,' she repeated. 'The Witches' Moon.'

'That was it!' said the big man. 'I remember now. That was the last line. 'Across the face of the Witches' Moon'.'

'Perhaps it's only a coincidence,' she muttered, 'but there's a place called the Witches' Moon about three miles from here, beyond Mallington.'

Mr. Budd became suddenly alert. 'What sort of a place, miss?' he asked quickly.

'An old inn,' she replied. 'It's nearly tumbling down now, and hasn't been used for years, not since the old post road was closed.'

'And it's called the Witches' Moon, miss?' said the big man.

'Yes. It's got a queer reputation in the district. Nobody will go near it — even in the daytime.'

'It's a queer name,' said Mr. Budd, stroking his cheek.

'Yes, isn't it,' said the woman. 'That's why I remembered. But it dates back well into the seventeenth century, I believe, and got its name then.'

'It's queer, as you say,' muttered Mr. Budd. 'That verse certainly mentioned the Witches' Moon, but it wasn't referrin' to this inn. Maybe, however, that's why someone had scrawled it on the flyleaf of that book. I'm glad you mentioned it, miss.'

'It may only be a coincidence,' she said doubtfully.

'It may,' he agreed, 'but I'm goin' to follow it up, all the same. Now I think you'd better be gettin' back to bed, miss.'

She acquiesced, and followed him into the hall. The air had suddenly grown very chill, and there was a draught somewhere that flickered the flame of the candle. They moved up the big staircase in silence, reached the landing and turned into the corridor that led to the woman's room. They had to pass the bedroom in which Krayle had died, but the door was closed.

Acting on a sudden impulse, Mr. Budd paused and tried the handle. To his surprise the door opened under his touch, and yet he remembered locking it and taking away the second key!

'What is it? What's the matter?' whispered Cathleen fearfully as she heard his exclamation.

But he made no answer. The light of his torch was flashing hither and thither about the darkened room. He saw something, reached up his hand and switched on the light to make sure.

And then he frowned. The book was back again on the bedside table. But the fireman's helmet which he remembered placing on the seat of the easy chair near the grate had vanished!

For a moment he stared, scarcely able to believe the evidence of his eyes. But there was no mistake. The book was there and the helmet had gone.

'What *is* happening in this house?' he muttered.

'What is it?' said Cathleen huskily, at his elbow.

He showed her, and her eyes widened. 'But why? What does it mean?' she asked.

He made a gesture of despair. 'Ask me another!' he muttered. She was shaking violently, and he took her arm and led her gently away. 'The best thing you can do, miss, is to go back to bed,' he said. 'You can do no good, and if you're not careful you'll catch your death of cold.'

She allowed herself to be taken over to the door of her room. 'I wish I'd never come here!' she whispered. 'I'm beginning to feel — afraid.'

'Don't you lose your nerve, miss,' said the superintendent kindly. 'No harm 'ull come to you. Just you go and have a good sleep.'

Her 'good night' was almost inaudible,

and when she'd closed the door he turned and retraced his steps to the death room. Who had visited it during the night, replaced the book, and taken the helmet? And why?

Wearily he passed a hand across the top of his head, smoothing his thinning hair. Here were two dead men — shot down in cold blood with an interval of three years between them, and not the slightest connecting link, so far as he could see, except that the dead men had been acquainted and that the crime had been committed under similar circumstances. And somewhere in the background lurked the vague possibility of a third murder by the same hand — the murder of Dench.

He yawned. Standing here in the middle of the night in an empty bedroom was not likely to help. He wished now that he had not sent the constable away. The man's presence would at least have put a stop to this midnight prowling on the part of someone. But Tipman was short-handed, and it had seemed unnecessary while he himself was in the house.

Maybe, he thought, as he put out the light and prepared to return to his interrupted rest, Cathleen Marsh's suggestion might yield something. The name of the ruined inn and the last line of that verse must be more than a coincidence. Perhaps there was something at the place that would give him a clue.

He climbed the stairs wearily and entered his bedroom, took off his dressing gown, and got heavily into bed. He was very tired, but his thoughts kept him awake for some time. But presently his eyes closed, his breathing grew deeper, and he slept.

The darkness of the house gradually changed to a pale, sooty grey as the windows began to take on shape. Dawn was approaching. In the silence there came presently the faintest of faint sounds, and among the gloomy shadows of the stairway moved a darker shadow, cautiously, stealthily. It began to creep down to the hall, a noiseless shape that paused at every second step to listen.

It reached the ground floor, stopped again, motionless, looking this way and that, and then went over to the stand where the outer coats and hats were hanging. Softly and without a sound, a heavy overcoat and a hat were taken down from a peg and put on, and the man moved over to the front door . . .

6

Exit Devine

Mr. Budd was wakened by a hand shaking him gently by the shoulder, and blinking sleepily up he saw the yellow face of Pullman standing over him.

'I'm sorry to disturb you, sir,' said the butler, 'but Miss Marsh thought you ought to know.'

'Know? Know what?' yawned Mr. Budd wearily as he struggled up on to one elbow.

'Mr. Devine, sir,' said Pullman. 'He's gone!'

'Gone!' echoed the superintendent. 'What d'you mean?'

'When I went to take him his tea I found the bed hadn't been slept in, and he's nowhere in the house. His overcoat and hat have gone, too.'

In spite of the tiredness which his disturbed night had left, the detective was instantly alert. 'Does anybody else know about this?' he asked.

'No, sir,' said Pullman, shaking his head. 'I only told Miss Marsh.'

'Then keep it to yourself!' ordered Mr. Budd. 'I'll get up at once!'

The old man shuffled away, and with a groan the superintendent hoisted himself out of bed. What did this new development mean? That Devine was the killer and that his nerve had failed him?

He gulped down the hot tea which Pullman had placed on the table by his bedside, went over to the wash-basin, filled it with cold water, and sluiced his face and hands. By the time he had hurriedly pulled on his clothes he was feeling less weary.

Pullman was in the hall talking to Cathleen Marsh. The woman, fully dressed, greeted him with a queer expression. 'Well,' she said quietly, 'the mystery is solved.'

'Is it, miss?' murmured Mr. Budd. 'Maybe we've merely been given another one.'

'What other explanation is there?' she

asked. 'Unless he was guilty, why should George Devine have run away?'

'Why should he have run away if he *was* guilty?' the big man said. 'There was nothin' against him. By runnin' away he's directin' suspicion on himself. It doesn't seem natural to me.'

'Well, there it is,' she said. 'He's gone!'

'How did he get out?' asked Mr. Budd.

She pointed towards the front door. 'We found it unbolted and the chain off this morning,' she said.

He frowned, massaging his chin. He couldn't reconcile the coolness of the murderer's previous actions with this sudden panic. Still, one never knew. Maybe he had lost his nerve and made up his mind that flight was the only thing left.

'Have you told his wife, miss?' he asked.

'No. I haven't told her yet,' Cathleen said. 'Nobody knows but you and me and Pullman.'

'And you think that he's the murderer?' murmured the detective doubtfully.

'If he's not, why did he go?' demanded

the woman. 'To leave in the night like that? What other reason could he have?'

'It's extraordinary, all the same,' said Mr. Budd. 'If he'd stayed there was no evidence against him.'

'Not so far as we know,' she said quickly. 'But he may have thought there was. Perhaps there was something that he thought we knew that we don't.'

'Well,' Mr. Budd remarked at length, 'he won't get very far.' He looked at the clock. It was a little after eight. 'Pity you haven't got a telephone here, miss,' he sighed wearily. 'Still, I'll have to make the best of it. Maybe you've got a car you can lend me?'

'There's Mr. Rutherford's,' said the woman. 'It's in the garage. Pullman will take you round.'

'Lock the door of Devine's room and keep the key, miss,' said Mr. Budd as he prepared to follow the butler. 'Not that keys seem to be much use in this house,' he added despondently.

The lawyer's car was a powerful one, and the big man found himself at the station house at Mallington at a quarter to nine. Inspector Tipman had just arrived, and he received the superintendent in his tiny office.

Mr. Budd explained the object of his mission, and Tipman listened with frowning brows. 'That looks as if he was our man,' he said. 'Well, we'll soon have him if he is.' He pulled the telephone towards him, lifted the receiver, and twenty minutes later a description of Devine, with instructions to detain him, was being broadcast to every police station in the country.

'He's a conspicuous-lookin' feller,' remarked the detective when this had been done. 'There shouldn't be much difficulty in pulling him in.'

'Oh we'll have him!' declared Tipman confidently. 'Probably before the day's out. I wonder what his motive was?' he added curiously.

'For clearin' off, d'you mean?' inquired Mr. Budd.

'No, for killing Marsh and this other man,' said Tipman.

'I wonder if he did kill 'em?' remarked the superintendent thoughtfully, and the inspector stared at him.

'Why should he have cleared off like this unless he was guilty?'

'That's what I'm wondering,' said Mr. Budd. 'I'm not at all satisfied that he cleared off because he was guilty.'

He left the inspector to digest this at his leisure, and went back to Wildcroft Manor.

The rest of the household were up when he arrived, and the men were assembled in the lounge.

'What's all this about, Devine?' demanded Gerald Trainor harshly as Mr. Budd came into the room. 'I hear he's escaped.'

'How did you hear that?' asked the big man sleepily.

'Is it true?' Trainor snapped.

'Well, he's gone, certainly,' admitted Mr. Budd.

'Then he must have been — ' began Trainor, and left the sentence unfinished, but they knew what he meant.

'It couldn't have been Devine!' said Curtis in his lazy drawl. 'It's impossible!'

'Why?' demanded Lionel Hope. 'If you ask me, it looks remarkably suspicious, his going off like this. You must admit that — as though he thought things were getting too warm for him.'

'How did you know he'd gone?' inquired Mr. Budd softly.

'I overheard Pullman talking to Miss Marsh,' said Trainor impatiently. 'Does it matter how we knew he'd gone?'

'Who's gone? Who are you talking about?' Alice Devine came quickly into the room and there was an uneasy silence. 'Who's gone?' she demanded again in a shrill, unpleasant voice.

'I'm afraid your husband has, ma'am,' answered Mr. Budd, and she caught her breath.

'Gone?' she said. 'What do you mean — gone?'

'He left sometime during the night,' explained the superintendent, and she swayed.

'Oh, my God!' she whispered brokenly. 'What did he want to go for? Leaving me here all by myself in this horrible house! I — ' She gave a little choking sob and collapsed, sliding out of Mr. Budd's supporting arm to the floor.

'She's fainted!' muttered Rutherford.

'Get some water, somebody!'

They lifted the senseless woman onto the settee while Trainor hurried to fetch water. In a little while her eyelashes twitched and she opened her eyes. For a moment she looked vacantly up at them, and then pushed herself to a sitting position.

'Gone!' she muttered weakly, and the tears began to run sluggishly down her cheeks. 'He shouldn't have gone! He ought to have had more consideration. Cathleen! Where's Cathleen?' she sobbed. 'It's her fault. All her fault! What did she bring us to this beastly place for?'

'What's the matter? What's happened?' Cathleen came quickly in, her face anxious and worried.

'George has gone, and it's your fault!' wailed the woman. 'What did you want to ask us here for?'

'You needn't have come,' said the woman coolly.

'You knew we'd come!' cried Alice Devine through her tears. 'You knew we'd come! We had to come!' She fished an inadequate handkerchief out of her pocket and dabbed at her eyes.

Mr. Budd felt a touch on his arm and Rutherford drew him to one side. 'Do you think this is the explanation?' whispered the lawyer.

'The explanation of what, sir?' demanded the big man a little irritably. He was tired and perplexed, and in no mood to answer questions.

'Of everything,' said Rutherford. 'Devine must have been guilty, or he wouldn't have bolted — '

'That's what everybody seems to think,' grunted Mr. Budd wearily.

'But you don't, eh?' The lawyer's eyes searched his questioningly.

'I don't think anythin',' said the superintendent. 'I've got beyond thinkin'. Tell me somethin'. Did Marsh use this place a lot?'

'A fair amount,' replied the lawyer in faint surprise. 'He was very fond of it. Sometimes he would spend weeks here, mostly in the summer, of course.'

'Thank you,' said Mr. Budd, and Rutherford looked at him curiously.

'Why did you ask that?' he inquired.

'Just out of curiosity,' answered the

detective, and his tone was noncommittal.

'Meaning,' said the lawyer, 'that you won't tell me. Well — '

He broke off as Pullman came hastily into the room. The butler was carrying an envelope in his hand, and approaching Cathleen Marsh he held it out. 'I've just found this, miss,' he said, 'in the hall. It had slipped down behind the coat rack.'

The woman took it and looked at the superscription with frowning brows. 'It's addressed to me,' she said wonderingly. 'What — '

'It's George's writing!' Alice Devine had struggled up from the settee and was peering curiously at the envelope. 'It's George's writing! What does he say? See what he says!'

Cathleen slid her thumb beneath the flap and drew out a single sheet of paper. Quickly she glanced at it, and Mr. Budd, who had left Rutherford and come to her side, read the hurried scrawl over her shoulder. It began abruptly:

'*Krayle knew something. He had some papers hidden away in a safe deposit. He told me before he died. I'm going to try* and find them. *Look after Alice.*'

Two initials that might have been anything ended the short message.

'So that's why he went,' murmured Mr. Budd. 'And that's why Krayle was killed.'

'What do you mean? What does it say?' cried Alice Devine shrilly.

The big man took the note from Cathleen's hand and read it aloud slowly. 'Krayle knew somethin',' he said. 'And what he knew he'd written down. And because of that he was killed.'

'You — you think he knew who shot my father?' whispered the woman.

'Yes, I do,' replied Mr. Budd, folding the letter and putting it in his pocket. 'He knew, and the murderer knew he knew.'

'So did Devine,' muttered Leslie Curtis significantly.

'Yes, sir,' agreed the superintendent. 'As you say, so did Mr. Devine.'

* * *

Breakfast that morning was a gloomy meal. Strangely enough, the disappearance of Devine seemed to have caused

122

greater consternation and uneasiness than had the murder of Krayle.

Eyeing the silent assembly gathered round the long table, Mr. Budd wondered what these people were concealing. Three years ago, when he had come to investigate the murder of Hebert Marsh, he had experienced the same thing. What was the secret they all shared and guarded so carefully? If he discovered it, it would be due to his own unaided efforts; there would be no help from them forthcoming. Of all these people, Cathleen Marsh was the only one he could rely on for assistance.

The meal came to an end. Trainor, Curtis and Rutherford went back to the lounge and grouped themselves round the fire. Lionel Hope, who seemed scarcely ever to speak, and only put in an appearance at meal times, disappeared, presumably to his bedroom.

Alice Devine, her eyes still red and puffy, announced her intention of lying down, and also went upstairs. Emily Marsh was still invisible. She had refused the big man's request for an interview on the plea that she was not feeling well enough, and for the time being he had, perforce, to accept it.

Sergeant Leek put in a belated appearance, apologetically explaining that he had overslept. Mr. Budd grunted. 'You could have come without wakin' up,' he said. 'Nobody would have noticed the difference! Now listen, I've got a job for you.' As concisely as possible he explained what had happened during the night. 'I want you,' he went on, 'to make a search for this helmet. It was taken by one of the people in the house, and unless Devine carried it away with him it's still here. I want to find it. I think it's important!'

'I don't see what anyone 'ud want a fireman's 'elmet for — ' began Leek argumentatively.

'Never mind what you see or what you don't see!' snapped Mr. Budd. 'You just do as you're told, will you!'

The sergeant sighed. 'I was only tryin' to tell you 'ow it struck me,' he protested lugubriously.

'Well, if you think it isn't important,' said Mr. Budd, 'it's probably the most important thing in the case! So you just try and find it. And remember, while I'm gone none of these people are to leave the house. You've got authority to see they don't — use it!'

'Are you goin' out?' asked the sergeant. 'Where are you goin' to?'

'Never mind where I'm goin' to!' said his superior. 'You've got your instructions, and that's all you need worry about.'

The morning was chill and damp when he left the house. Although it was not actually raining, the sky, grey and sombre, looked as if rain was not very far off.

The big man made his way to the police station at Mallington, and for the second time that day interviewed Inspector Tipman. The inspector eyed him in surprise when he put his question.

'The Witches' Moon?' he said. 'Yes, I know it. On the outskirts of Devil's Wood. Is that the place you mean?'

'If it's called the Witches' Moon that's the place I mean,' agreed Mr. Budd. 'How do I get to it?'

Tipman explained, augmenting his

explanation with a rough plan which he drew on his blotting pad. 'You can't miss it,' he concluded. 'Once you come out of Devil's Wood the place is about a hundred yards to the right along the old post road.'

Mr. Budd examined the rough sketch carefully. 'I'll find it all right,' he said.

'What d'you want to go there for?' demanded the inspector. 'The place is almost falling to pieces. It hasn't been used for years. Why they haven't pulled it down long ago beats me.'

'Who does it belong to?' asked the big man.

'Well, I don't know as I can rightly tell you,' replied the inspector. 'I suppose it's private property. Everybody avoids it round here. It was abandoned suddenly, years ago. There was some scare or other, and everybody cleared out at a moment's notice. Nobody's ever been back.

'I've never thought much about it, but I've heard a lot of gossip. There used to be a good deal of superstition about this place, Kings Mailing in particular. Supposed to have been a centre for black magic and witchcraft and such things. The Devil's Wood is one of the places where, in the old days, the witches were supposed to meet Old Nick and hold their sabbaths. Lot of rubbish, of course, but you know how these sort of things stick. There's few people in the district, particularly among the older inhabitants, who'd go near the wood or the Witches' Moon after dark, and some of 'em not even in daylight.'

'Sounds an interestin' place,' remarked Mr. Budd. 'I'll go and have a look at it. I'm interested in old buildin's.'

He took his departure, leaving Inspector Tipman's curiosity unsatisfied. He had no difficulty in finding his way, for Tipman's directions had been explicit.

Devil's Wood was a thick plantation in which the trees grew so closely together that in spite of their leafless condition the grey light of day scarcely penetrated the closely interwoven branches. It was a gloomy place enough, with its rotting bracken and tangled undergrowth, and the big man was not surprised that the inhabitants of the surrounding district looked on it with suspicion and gave it a wide berth. If one believed in such things, it was possible to imagine that it might have been used in olden times for the unholy rites with which legend had associated it. In spite of his practical and phlegmatic nature, Mr. Budd experienced a sense of relief when he emerged from that cheerless and desolate strip of woodland.

Following the directions, which he had memorised, he turned to the right, and a few moments later got his first glimpse of the Witches' Moon. It stood well back from the roadway, surrounded by a dense belt of trees that were so thick that they presented the appearance of solid blackness. It was a low, rambling building of heavy timbers and dilapidated roofing, a portion of which had fallen away, leaving a gaping hole; the entire place was overgrown by the bushes which had sprung up unchecked around it, and from which projected the post on which swung the creaking and time-obliterated sign.

The superintendent paused and took stock of the building from the roadway. In the melancholy grey of that October day it looked uninviting enough — a derelict, neglected and forgotten, thrown up by the waves of time to rot upon the beach of progress. What connection was there between this abandoned ruin and the queer happenings at Wildcroft Manor? It must be something more than a coincidence that the last three words of the verse in that book on Krayle's bedside table should be identical to the name of the place which he was now looking at. But what exactly did it signify?

Mr. Budd picked his way through the wild profusion of weeds and bushes around the place, and presently found himself standing in the shadow of the crumbling and decaying porch. The blistered, paintless door opened under the pressure of his hand and he peered into the semi-darkness of the interior. A smell of age and corruption; of rotting wood and dampness, greeted him.

He entered, and presently, as his eyes grew accustomed to the gloom, saw that he was standing in a wide, bare entrance hall with a low ceiling of heavy beams. A door to his left was open and he saw that it had originally led to the bar. He also saw something else at the same moment. The floor was strewn thickly with sawdust.

Sawdust!

His mind went back swiftly to that morning when he had stood in the mortuary with Inspector Tipman and gazed down at the body of James Augustus Dench. Was this the place to which he had been brought? Was it here that he had met his death?

The stout man closed the door and went into the bar. Ancient barrels lined the walls and there was a faint, stale smell of beer. The shelves behind the rotting counter were laden with dust-covered bottles. On the bar itself stood a group of grimy glasses.

The place was panelled with aged oak. There was an oak settle, a table and a broken chair. The floor round the wainscoting was riddled with rat holes, and over everything was a grey film, the dust of years.

Mr. Budd glanced quickly round and

came out into the passage. There was another door just beyond the one that led into the bar, and this was closed. Opening it, he found himself in a smaller room which he concluded must originally have been the bar-parlour. This, too, was panelled in worm-eaten oak. A fireplace of undressed bricks faced the doorway and above it was a carving which instantly attracted his attention. As a work of art it was crude, but the craftsman had, in some devilish manner, caught the very spirit of his subject: a windswept tract of country, bathed in the rays of a full moon, which hung low in the sky; and across it, sweeping down towards the fringe of a dense wood, a flying army of witches! There was life in the trailing garments that floated out behind them as they came out of the night sky; life in the demoniacal, distorted faces, alight with anticipation of the orgies to come; life in the whole weird conception which even age and the covering grime could not destroy.

Mr. Budd stared at the carven picture and concluded that it was not the sort of thing he would have liked in his own house. His tastes ran more in the direction of 'The Monarch of the Glen', or perhaps 'And When Did You Last See Your Father?', reproductions of which graced the walls of his Streatham villa. Still, considering the name of the place, no doubt this was a suitable decoration.

However, he hadn't come to find such things as that. His business was to discover if there were any connection between this place and the murders of Krayle and Dench.

He looked about him, but there was nothing to be seen here, any more than there had been in the bar. He explored the whole of the ground floor and what was left of the upper storey. Then passing through a large, stone-flagged kitchen, he came to a smaller room that had evidently been a kind of scullery/wash-house. Among the accumulated litter on the floor he discovered a rusty iron ring, and concluded that it was the entrance to the cellar. Stooping, he gripped it and pulled. A large wooden trap opened, revealing the top of a broken flight of steps, the bottom of which disappeared into darkness. He took his torch from his pocket and flashed the light through the hole; and then, carefully testing the steps, he began to descend gingerly into the depths.

Presently he found himself in a big low-roofed vault, the ceiling of which was supported by square brick pillars. It looked as if it extended completely under the building, and was lined with huge wine barrels and bins. The floor was thick with dirt and grime, and in one corner was a pile of empty bottles. But it was the heap of blankets against one pillar that caught and held his attention, for they were new, and, in comparison with the rest of the place, clean.

Near to them, on an upturned crate, was a candle stuck in a bottle; beside it were a dirty cracked plate and a cup. Mr. Budd went over and looked down. Was this the place where Dench had been kept prisoner? Had this been his bed?

He began to examine the vault-like chamber, flashing his torch from side to side; and presently he stopped, focused it on a spot on the floor, and stared at the circle of light. Here the stone of the floor was darkened by an irregular patch that was not slime. It was surrounded by several other splashes, and there was no need to look twice to see that they were congealed blood!

It was here, then, that James Augustus Dench had been killed, and any remaining doubt that Mr. Budd may have had that his murder was mixed up with the deaths of Hebert Marsh and John Krayle was dispelled at that moment.

7

The Ottoman

It was late in the afternoon when Mr. Budd returned to Wildcroft Manor. After his discovery at the abandoned inn, he had left everything as he had found it and returned to Mallington to acquaint a startled and surprised Tipman with the result of his visit to the Witches' Moon.

'How did you know that Dench had been killed there?' demanded the inspector.

'I didn't know,' said Mr. Budd truthfully, 'but I know now. Keep this to yourself. At the present moment I don't think we'd be wise to make it public. I'd like you to put a man on to guard the place.'

'Yes, I'll see to that,' said the inspector. 'But if you didn't know what you were going to find, what made you go there?'

'You remember that verse on the flyleaf of the book in Krayle's bedroom?' said the stout man, and Tipman uttered an exclamation.

'Of course!' he said. 'But I never connected it with the ruined inn.'

'Neither did I,' said Mr. Budd, 'for the simple reason I didn't know anythin' about the ruined inn. It was Miss Marsh who put me wise.'

'But what I can't understand,' said the inspector, 'is how Dench's murder links up with this other business.'

'I'm not surprised,' murmured the detective. 'I don't understand it meself. But it's pretty evident it does. Maybe we're goin' to understand a lot later.'

He left the puzzled inspector, found a small pub, and settled himself down to a lunch of bread and cheese and beer. He had no relish for another meal in the taciturn and suspicious society at the manor, preferring his own company and his thoughts. When he finally reached the big house, Leek had a negative report.

'I've searched everywhere,' said the sergeant, 'but there's no sign of that 'elmet. It ain't in the 'ouse, I'm sure of that!'

'You've looked in all the rooms?' said Mr. Budd.

'All except the old woman's,' answered the sergeant. 'I couldn't go in there because she's been there all day. But I should 'ardly think she'd 'ave it.'

'You hardly think anyway!' grunted his superior, and left him to find Cathleen. He discovered the woman in the kitchen.

'D'you think I could see your aunt this afternoon, miss?' he asked.

'I'll try and arrange it,' she said. 'You may find her a little . . . difficult, though,' she added with a smile.

'I'll risk that,' said Mr. Budd. 'I'm used to dealin' with difficult people.'

He hurried away, and Pullman, who was cleaning some silver, raised his yellow face. 'Excuse me, sir,' he said hesitantly, 'but — but do you think Mr. Devine was responsible for — for all this?'

'What do *you* think?' asked Mr. Budd.

'I — I don't know what to think,' the butler stammered. 'It's funny 'e should 'ave gone off like that — if 'e *did* go,' he added under his breath.

The stout man's eyes narrowed. 'What

do you mean by that?' he inquired softly.

'I meant — well, I didn't mean anything, sir.' Pullman tried to meet his steady gaze, but dropped his eyes.

'Pullman,' said Mr. Budd softly, 'what do you know?'

'Know, sir?' The butler licked his lips. 'I don't understand what you mean, sir. Know about what?'

'About this affair!' snapped the superintendent, and then, as the man opened his mouth: 'Come on, you know somethin' that you haven't told. What is it?'

Pullman shook his bald head. 'I know nothing about it, sir!' he declared emphatically.

'You may not know who did the actual murders,' persisted Mr. Budd, 'but you know somethin'. Now come on, out with it!'

'I know nothing, sir!' repeated the butler stubbornly.

The big man checked an angry exclamation. The same from everybody, even the servants. A barrier of lies that he was powerless to break down. He knew all these people were hiding something, had known it three years ago, but he had no

138

tangible proof, could not openly accuse them of concealing anything. Never before had he come up against such a concerted attempt to hide the truth.

'Now listen here, Pullman,' he said, 'you're hidin' somethin' — everybody in this house is hidin' somethin' — and it won't do any of you any good in the long run. I'm goin' to find out the truth, and find it out I will.'

'The truth is sometimes very — very ugly, sir,' murmured the butler.

'Now just what do you mean by that?' snapped Mr. Budd.

Pullman looked at him queerly. 'I know nothing, sir,' he said. 'I told you that before. Please remember that *I know nothing*. But two men have been killed. Why not let it rest there, sir.'

'I see!' Mr. Budd nodded gently. 'So we've got to let this killer get away with it, eh?'

'If you could be sure that the guilty person would be the only one to suffer, it would be different,' answered Pullman. 'But supposing finding the guilty person was going to make others who were innocent suffer. What then, sir?'

Before Mr. Budd could reply, Cathleen came back. 'My aunt will see you,' she said. 'She's in her room.'

He thanked her, and followed her to the door. 'Miss Marsh,' he said as they crossed the hall, 'what is everyone in this house afraid of?'

'So you've noticed that?' she asked.

'Nobody could help but notice it,' said the big man. 'I noticed it at the time your father was killed.'

'I don't know.' She shook her head. 'I don't know, but it's true. Everyone — everyone seems to be afraid of the truth coming out.'

'I think you're right,' he answered.

'But we've got to find out all the same,' said the woman determinedly. 'We've *got* to. I must know!'

Again he wondered why she was so anxious after such a lapse of time, but she had left him before he could put the question.

Making his way up the stairs, he paused outside Emily Marsh's room and tapped on the door.

'Come in,' called a harsh, strident voice, and he entered.

The old woman was lying on the bed, propped up with pillows and covered with a quilt. Her eyes glared at him malevolently. 'Well, what do you want with me?' she demanded.

'Only to ask you a few questions, ma'am,' said Mr. Budd, and she made an impatient gesture.

'Questions! Nothing but questions!' she grated. 'Didn't you ask enough questions three years ago?'

'Apparently I didn't, ma'am,' retorted the detective. 'Otherwise I might have known enough to prevent what's just happened!'

'Well, what do you want to ask me?' she said curtly. 'Why stir up a muddy pool? Why not leave it?'

'I'm surprised at your attitude, ma'am. Surely you're as anxious as anyone to clear up this business?'

'No!'

The word was like a shot from a gun, and he was staggered at the intensity of feeling that lay behind it. 'But why, ma'am?' he said.

'Because no good and much harm may come from it,' said the woman. 'Herbert's dead, Krayle's dead. Nothing can restore them to life. Let the dead rest in peace, and the living also!'

'Even if one of the living's a murderer?' said Mr. Budd, and she nodded.

'Even so!' she said.

'I'm afraid I can't do that, ma'am,' answered the big man. 'I've got my duty to perform, and I must do it.'

'Well, you can expect no help from me,' she muttered. 'Neither you nor anyone else can force me to speak if I don't want to! I consented to see you to tell you that. Now go and leave me alone!'

On this unsatisfactory note the interview terminated. Mr. Budd, rendered irritable and bad-tempered by this continued conspiracy of silence, returned downstairs. The lugubrious Leek was standing rather dejectedly in the hall, and the stout man signalled to him.

'Now listen here,' he said when the sergeant had followed him into the dining room, 'I'm goin' to arrange with Miss

Marsh for you to stop here tonight.' Leek's long face expressed anything but pleasure at the news.

'Oh, are you?' he said. 'D'you think it's necessary?'

'If it wasn't necessary I shouldn't do it!' snapped Mr. Budd. 'I'm not riskin' anybody prowling about again and perhaps scootin' off while we're all asleep. So we'll take it in turns to watch. I'll stay up until four and you can relieve me then and keep watch until the mornin'.'

Leek thought of his comfortable bed in the little cottage where he had been staying, and greeted the arrangement without enthusiasm.

'You can have my bed,' went on Mr. Budd, 'so there won't be any need to put Miss Marsh to any trouble.'

'Who d'you think is goin' to try and bolt?' asked the sergeant.

'I don't think anybody's goin' to try an' 'bolt',' answered his superior, 'because I'm not goin' to give 'em a chance to try, see?'

He mentioned his suggestion to Cathleen Marsh later, and she made no demur.

'Sergeant Leek can have Mr. Devine's room, if you like,' she said.

'I think he'll be all right in mine, miss,' replied Mr. Budd. 'I can make sure he wakes up then, when it's time for me to go to bed.' After dinner he went down to the police station to enquire if any news had come in concerning the missing Devine. But nothing had arrived.

'It's rather queer,' said Tipman. 'There seems to be no trace of him at all. I should have thought it would have been easy to pick him up.'

'Yes, so should I,' agreed Mr. Budd, and the lack of news made him feel vaguely uneasy. Supposing Devine was not the murderer? Then after that letter, the real murderer would know there was a safe deposit somewhere, rented by Krayle, which contained proof of his guilt. He'd strain every nerve to destroy that proof.

On his way back to the manor, the superintendent began to wonder if George Devine *had* gone, as everyone thought. If the killer of Dench, Marsh and Krayle was aware that Devine knew the whereabouts of this safe deposit, would he have permitted him to leave?

He was still turning this thought over in his mind when he came into the lounge. It was warm and cosy after the coldness of the night, and with the leaping fire and the soft lights, presented an agreeable contrast to the darkness without. The lean form of Leek was perched uncomfortably on a chair in one corner, watching the four men near the fire as they played a desultory hand of bridge.

Cathleen was sewing quietly, and Alice Devine, curled up on the settee, was reading. They all looked up as Mr. Budd entered, but nobody said anything; and as the big man crossed ponderously to the fire, they continued their various occupations. He was warming his hands when Pullman came in from the kitchen.

'Excuse me, miss,' he said, addressing Cathleen, 'but have you got a piece of string? We've hunted high and low for a piece in the kitchen and there ain't any.'

'String?' said the woman. 'I don't know. You'd better look in the ottoman. We used to keep odds and ends in there, didn't we?'

'Yes, miss. I remembered that,' said the butler, and crossed over to the long padded seat that ran beneath the window. He shifted the cushions and opened the top, and his scream brought everybody to their feet with bloodless faces.

'What is it?' snarled Mr. Budd.

'Oh, my God!' whispered the butler with chattering teeth. 'Oh my God — ' he mouthed soundlessly, his yellow face the colour of putty, stabbing with a shaking finger at the open ottoman.

Mr. Budd went swiftly over, and one glance showed him the cause of the butler's fear. In the narrow, box-like compartment lay George Devine! He was quite dead, and on the breast of his waistcoat, visible between the opening of the jacket and overcoat, was a dark, irregular patch of dried blood.

*　*　*

It's not surprisin' we couldn't trace 'im,' said Inspector Tipman two hours later, as he stood talking to Mr. Budd in the empty lounge. 'It's pretty evident he never left the house at all.'

'I was beginnin' to get rather afraid somethin' like this had happened,' the big man murmured, 'when no news came through. It was next to impossible that a feller like Devine could have escaped notice when there was a hue and cry after him.' He shook his head with a worried frown. 'Four people killed,' he said. 'And we're no nearer to findin' out who did it than we were three years ago.'

Immediately after the discovery in the ottoman he had dispatched Leek to the police station at Mallington to notify Tipman. The inspector had arrived, accompanied by the police doctor and Sergeant Wishit. Devine's body had been lifted out of its resting place, and the doctor — it was the same man who had examined Krayle and reminded Mr. Budd of Crippen — made his examination.

His report was brief. The dead man had been stabbed, and as near as he could tell had been dead about fourteen hours. Without an autopsy he was not prepared to be more definite than this. There was no sign of the weapon, but Devine had obviously been prepared to leave the house when he had met his death, for he was fully dressed, and his hat was discovered crushed under his body.

Alice Devine had completely collapsed from the shock, and was in such a state that Mr. Budd had sent the doctor to see her. He reported that there was nothing serious the matter with her, only hysteria, and that the best thing she could do was to remain in bed and keep quiet.

The ambulance came and removed Devine's body, and when this had been attended to Tipman had called the rest of the household into the dining room; and in company with Mr. Budd, he once more closely questioned them — without, however, eliciting anything helpful.

The atmosphere of fear and terror had increased with this fresh tragedy, and everyone looked pinched and strained. Cathleen Marsh, in particular, appeared to be suffering acutely from this latest calamity. She insisted over and over again that it was all her fault; that but for her wild idea it would never have happened.

Mr. Budd tried to console her as best

he could, but his words had little effect; her spirit seemed to have been crushed.

'It must have been one of these people,' said Tipman, 'but the question is — which?'

'That *is* the question,' answered Mr. Budd. 'And the answer to it lies in that safe deposit of Krayle's. We've got to find that, and find it before the murderer does.'

'If it exists,' muttered the inspector sceptically.

'Oh, it exists all right,' said the superintendent. 'Krayle was killed because it existed. This poor feller Devine was killed because it existed. I'll get the Yard to attend to that. They can set inquiries round at all the likely places.' He rubbed his ample chin thoughtfully. 'Whoever the murderer is, he's a pretty cool hand,' he went on after a pause. 'And desperate. He's killin' now to save his own skin. I wonder who'll be next.'

The startled Tipman stared at him. 'Good Lord!' he exclaimed. 'You don't expect any more, do you?'

'If there's anybody else whose death will make this feller safe, they'll die!' declared Mr. Budd emphatically. 'Or an attempt will be made to kill 'em.'

'But the risk — ' began Tipman.

'The risk will not stop him,' interrupted the big man. 'He loses nothin' by goin' on with his plans, and everythin' by not. If he's caught now he's bound to be hanged. Another murder or so won't affect his sentence, and may have the effect of making him perfectly safe. No, if another death 'ull help him he won't hesitate, that's certain.'

'Well, we'll have to find him before he can do any more damage,' said the inspector. 'Have you any suspicion?'

'Not the slightest!' said Mr. Budd, shaking his head.

'Well, it's someone inside the house, that's evident,' continued Tipman. 'Now who have we got? There's Pullman and the cook, Miss Hutton.' He checked them off on his fingers as he spoke. 'Miss Marsh and her aunt. Lionel Hope, Trainor, Rutherford, Mrs. Devine and Leslie Curtis. That's nine. I suppose we can eliminate Miss Marsh, so that's really only eight.'

'I'm eliminatin' nobody!' declared Mr. Budd. 'I'm pretty sure meself that Miss Marsh has got nothin' to do with it, but I'm not eliminatin' her until I've got convincin' proof. You've got to remember,' he went on, as Tipman remained silent, 'that it was her idea that started all this. If she hadn't reopened this house and brought all these people down, Krayle and Devine 'ud never have been killed.'

'No, that's true,' admitted the inspector. 'So we've got nine people to choose from.'

'One of nine!' murmured Mr. Budd. 'Which one, and why?' It was impossible to even conjecture. They might any of them be guilty, yes, even Miss Marsh, for there was abnormal cunning behind the affair. She might quite easily have invited him in order to divert suspicion from herself. Supposing, just for the sake of argument, it was Cathleen Marsh. What could be the motive?

Here he found himself up against a brick wall. That was the whole trouble with this case: there was no motive for anybody in particular. They had, apparently, all hated Hebert Marsh for some unknown reason; and yet, hating him, they had been content to spend weekends at his invitation. On the face of it, it seemed ridiculous. If they had all disliked the man so much, why accept his hospitality?

A sudden thought struck him, and it was such a simple solution that he wondered he'd not considered it before. Was there something that had *forced* them to accept Marsh's invitation? Some hold that the dead man had had over them? That seemed a plausible explanation, but where did it lead? Nowhere. Unless the hold he had had, if any, could be discovered. He mentioned this suggestion to Inspector Tipman.

'There may be something in it,' agreed the local man. 'But what I can't understand is how this fellow Dench comes into it. There seems to be a connection, but what I can't see.'

'No more can I,' said Mr. Budd. 'And that's not the only thing I can't see, either. You put that feller on to guard the Witches' Moon as I suggested?'

'Yes, I sent Hammond,' he answered. 'And he'll be relieved by Wullen. He didn't relish the job, I can tell you. What I'd like to know is — '

His desires were not destined to be made public, for at that moment Leek came hurriedly into the room. 'I've found the 'elmet!' he blurted, and Mr. Budd was instantly alert.

'Oh, you've found it, have you?' he said. 'Where?'

'I bet you'd never guess,' said the lean sergeant excitedly, and his superior made a gesture of impatience.

'I'm not goin' to try!' he snapped. 'This ain't a guessin' competition. Where did you find it?'

'In Devine's room,' answered Leek. 'Up the chimney!'

'Up the chimney?' repeated Mr. Budd, raising his eyebrows.

'I'd looked in the room before,' explained the sergeant. 'I wouldn't 'ave found it at all, only it fell down as I was walkin' across the floor.'

'In Devine's chimney, eh?' said Mr. Budd softly. 'Let me have a look at it.'

He took the helmet from Leek's hand and gazed at it sleepily. It was smeared with soot and there were scratches on the brass. Obviously it had been thrust hurriedly up the chimney, and the vibration of the sergeant's footsteps had dislodged it from its insecure resting place. So it had been Devine who had removed it from Krayle's room.

Brushing off the film of soot with his handkerchief, the superintendent carried the helmet over to a standard lamp, and under the light examined it carefully. But he could discover nothing that he had not previously seen. With the exception of the inscription, it was just an ordinary fireman's helmet.

He frowned thoughtfully while Leek and Inspector Tipman watched him. There must be something curious about the thing, otherwise why should Devine have gone to such trouble and risk to take it from the dead man's room and hide it in his own chimney?

'I think I'll go up to this feller's room

and have a look round,' he said after a pause. 'Maybe there's something there that'll tell us what he wanted this thing for.'

They accompanied him up the stairs and into the dead man's bedroom. In the empty grate was a mass of soot which the helmet had brought down with it. But except for that, the grate was clean. Standing in the centre of the apartment, the big man looked about him.

It was furnished much as the other rooms were, solidly and comfortably. A dressing table stood near the window, a tall-boy in one corner; and against the blank wall, opposite the fireplace, was the bed. There was a wardrobe behind the door, and opening this Mr. Budd stared inside. Two suits hung neatly on hangers, a grey tweed and a suit of evening clothes. Beside them was a woollen dressing gown. He lifted this down and ran through the pockets. In one of them he found a crumpled scrap of paper. Smoothing it out, he glanced at it and saw that it was covered with figures scrawled in pencil. A whole string of them.

'What have you found?' asked Tipman curiously.

Mr. Budd showed him.

'Looks as if he'd been doing some calculations,' said the inspector.

'Queer sort of calculations,' murmured the detective, wrinkling his brows. 'There's no sort of sum here, just a line of figures with a full stop between 'em.' He turned the paper over but the other side was blank. 'It may mean nothin' and it may mean a lot,' he went on. I've got a hunch it means a lot.'

He pursed his lips and stared once more at the line of numerals which ran: 7. 20. 2.14. 21. 3. 3. 14. 3. 14.15. 5. 2.17. 22.13. 7. 7. 46. 17. 15. 5.18. 5.10.7.

'Well, if you can make anything out of it you're cleverer than I am,' grunted Tipman.

Mr. Budd made no reply, but his lips moved as he silently repeated the numbers to himself. Suddenly he gave a grunt. 'Give me that helmet a minute,' he said.

Sergeant Leek, to whom he had entrusted it, held it out. The big man went over to the bed and sat down, laid the helmet beside him, and produced from his pocket a pencil and an old envelope. Rapidly he copied down the string of figures, and then turning the helmet so that he could read the inscription, he wrote this down also.

For some seconds he stared at the result with knitted brows, and then his face cleared and he began to work quickly.

Taking the first number, 7, he counted to the seventh letter of the inscription. It was T. The second number was 20, and he put down U beside the T.

In ten minutes he had a complete string of letters which ran: TURN-MOONONCERIGHTTWICELEFT.

With a little nod of satisfaction he proceeded to divide the jumble into words, and when he had done this the complete message appeared startlingly clear: TURN MOON ONCE RIGHT TWICE LEFT.

'You've got a car outside, haven't you?' he said quickly, looking up to Inspector Tipman. The local man nodded. 'Come on then,' said Mr. Budd. 'You can stop here, Leek, and see that nobody tries any funny business while we're away.'

'Where are you goin'?' demanded the sergeant.

'We're goin' to the Witches' Moon,' said his superior, 'to find out what happens when we carry out the instructions in this message!'

8

The Safe

The weather had changed. The chill dampness of the morning had given place to a hard frost, and a sliver of moon hung high in a cold sky. Its clear light bathed the ruined inn by the old post road, forming sharply contrasting shadows of dense blackness.

Complete silence surrounded the dilapidated building, a silence that was broken only by the faint far-away whistle of a locomotive; and there was no sign of life in the vicinity.

Mr. Budd and Inspector Tipman stopped before the forbidding exterior and eyed it without enthusiasm. 'Creepy-looking place, ain't it?' muttered Tipman. 'No wonder the people of the district keep away. You could imagine all sorts of unpleasant things happening here.'

'I expect they did in the days gone by,'

answered the big man. 'When you come across a place with an evil reputation there's always some basis for it. I wonder whereabouts your man is?'

'Round at the back I expect,' said the inspector. 'The rear part is in better repair than the rest.' They had been forced to leave the car at the beginning of the old road and traverse the rest of the way on foot. Crossing the bush-grown patch in front of the entrance, they reached the porch, and as they did so a burly figure appeared and hailed them.

'It's all right, Hammond,' said Tipman. 'It's me!'

The constable looked relieved. 'I 'eard somebody moving about and speakin', sir,' he said, 'and I wondered what was up. I don't mind tellin' you that I shan't be sorry when this job's over. This place gets on your nerves.'

'Nothin's happened, I suppose?' said Mr. Budd.

'No, nothing's happened, sir,' the policeman answered. 'But there's all sorts of queer noises. You could imagine anythin' in a place like this.'

He led the way into the musty passage, and conducted them along to the kitchen. It was much the same as when Mr. Budd had seen it before, except that there was a fire burning in the old range and an oil lamp stood on the rickety table.

'I've just finished me supper,' said Hammond, pointing to the remains of a meal. He looked from one to the other, evidently curious to know what had brought them to the old inn at that hour, for it was nearly midnight.

Mr. Budd answered the unspoken question. 'We've just come to have a look at the bar parlour,' he said. 'Can we borrow your lamp?'

'Yes, sir,' said the astonished policeman. 'You'll 'ave to be careful; it smokes a bit when you move it.'

The superintendent picked it up. 'You'd better come with us,' he said, and made his way along the draughty passage to the room in which he had previously seen the carving over the fireplace.

Inspector Tipman followed with the constable, looking about him disparagingly. 'I can't understand why the place is left standing,' he said as they entered the bar parlour. 'It's practically falling to pieces. Why don't they pull it down?'

'Probably because the owner objects,' murmured Mr. Budd. 'And that's a thing I'd like you to find out, Tipman. I'm very curious to know who this property belongs to.'

'It's a part of Sir Alfred Mowbury's estate, sir,' interjected the policeman. 'All this part of the country belongs to him, Devils Wood 'n' all.'

'Who's Sir Alfred Mowbury?' asked Mr. Budd.

'He lives up at the 'all, over at Seldon Magna,' said Hammond.

'And this place belongs to him, eh?' muttered the stout man. 'Well, if it belonged to me I know what I'd do with it. But different people have different ideas.'

He set the lamp down on a corner of the brick mantelpiece, and as its light illumined the carving Inspector Tipman whistled. 'Ugly-looking thing!' he remarked. 'So that's what the message refers to.'

'I'm hopin' so,' said Mr. Budd. 'But we'll soon know.' He produced the envelope on which he had jotted down the deciphered instructions. 'Turn moon once right twice left,' he murmured. 'It seems pretty obvious that must refer to the moon in the carvin'. Well, we'll see what happens.'

He dragged over a broken chair, tested it carefully to find out if it would support his weight, and climbing laboriously up found he was just able to touch the wooden disc. Gripping it by the edge with both hands, he twisted it to the right. It moved stiffly on a central pivot, and there was a faint click. Repeating the action to the left brought a like result, and on the second turn to the left Hammond uttered an amazed exclamation.

'Blimey, look at that!' he said in astonishment.

For a second nothing had happened; and then, with a slight rumbling noise, a panel at the side of the fireplace dropped down, disclosing a dark cavity beyond, about two feet square.

'Good Lord!' exclaimed Inspector Tipman. 'A secret panel!'

'Let's see what's behind it,' grunted

Mr. Budd, stepping gingerly down from his precarious perch. He took the lamp and held it so that it flooded the cavity. The panel had concealed the polished steel door of a safe.

Inspector Tipman's small, rather closely set eyes opened to their widest extent. 'A safe!' he exclaimed. Mr. Budd said nothing, but his brows drew together as he bent down. It was quite a small safe, and it had been stood in a cupboard-like compartment built in the thickness of the wall. The steel door was a little less than eighteen inches across, and the lock was a combination one. The dial was set at 0000.

'Queer thing to find in an old building like this,' murmured Mr. Budd softly.

'You're right!' agreed Tipman. 'I wonder how it got here?'

'I'm not good at guessin',' said the big man. 'But it's a long time since it was last used.' He pointed to where the steel was spotted here and there with rust. 'Well, we're gettin' nearer to the motive for Dench's murder.'

Tipman looked puzzled for a moment, and then a light of understanding came to his eyes. 'By gosh!' he exclaimed. 'Of course, he used to work in a safe-maker's!'

'Yes,' said Mr. Budd, nodding, 'and I wouldn't mind bettin' that this is one of their products. Dench was kidnapped by someone who wanted this safe opened, and when he wouldn't open it they killed him.'

'How d'you know he wouldn't open it?' demanded the inspector.

'Because nobody *has* opened it,' replied the stout man. 'You can see that for yourself. Look at the dust on the dial. It's been there longer than the time Dench has been dead. Either he couldn't open it or he wouldn't open it. But they had to kill him anyway, because he knew too much.'

An exclamation from the doorway made him swing round. Gerald Trainor was standing on the threshold, his face white, his eyes glaring. 'How did you find that?' he croaked. 'How long have you known it was there?'

Inspector Tipman eyed him suspiciously. 'How did you get here?' he demanded, but Trainor took no notice of the question.

'Have you opened it?' he said eagerly. 'Have you opened it?'

Mr. Budd inspected him curiously. The man was shaking with excitement. His face was haggard and drawn. Obviously the sight of the safe affected him strongly, but with what emotion it was difficult to guess. There was trace of surprise mingled with more than a trace of fear. Either he had not known of the safe's existence or he had never expected anyone to find it.

'We've not opened it yet, Mr. Trainor,' the superintendent said smoothly. 'Nobody but an expert can open it unless they know the combination.'

An expression of relief flitted over Trainor's face.

'I'd very much like to know,' continued Mr. Budd, 'what you're doin' here, sir?'

'I — I followed you,' answered the man hesitantly. 'I — I heard you say you were coming here and I was curious to know what for.'

'You were curious, eh?' said the superintendent. 'What do you know about this place, Mr. Trainor?'

'Nothing! Nothing!' answered Trainor quickly.

'I suppose,' said the superintendent, acting on a sudden thought that had just occurred to him, 'that this safe belonged to Hebert Marsh?'

The shot was a wild one, but it went home. Trainor started and licked his lips. 'I don't know,' he answered thickly, shaking his head. 'I don't know. I couldn't tell you. I've never seen it before. I'd no idea it was here. How did you find it? Who told you where to look?' He was labouring under the strain of some intense nervous excitement which rendered his speech staccato and disconnected.

'Nobody,' said Mr. Budd evasively. 'We found it by accident.' This was not strictly true, but he had no intention of taking the man before him into his confidence. 'It seems very peculiar to me,' he went on, 'that you should be so interested.'

'Naturally I'm interested,' said Trainor. 'Aren't we all interested? After what's happened, who could help it?'

It was an evasive answer, and it did not

satisfy Mr. Budd at all. 'I'd be glad if your interest 'ud lead you to be a little more candid, Mr. Trainor,' he said significantly, and a flush spread over Trainor's pale face.

'What d'you mean?' he demanded angrily. 'I don't know anything — '

'Nobody knows anythin',' sighed the detective sadly. 'They keep on sayin' so. They've said it so often that maybe they're beginning to believe it themselves.' He took a step forward and stared Trainor full in the face, and his usually sleepy eyes were hard. 'What are you all hidin' up?' he snapped suddenly. 'Why are you so afraid that the truth might come out?'

The other tried to return his gaze, but his eyes dropped. 'I don't know what you're talkin' about,' he muttered.

'You know very well what I'm talkin' about!' snarled the big man. 'Four people have been killed up to now and all because none of you has got the courage to speak out!'

'Four?' There was surprise in Trainor's voice.

'Yes, four!' said Mr. Budd. 'Hebert Marsh, John Krayle, George Devine, and Dench.'

The man before him was either a very good actor or he was genuinely astonished. 'Dench?' he echoed, the fear momentarily leaving his face. 'You mean the man who disappeared and was found dead in a tunnel?'

'I don't know of any other Dench,' murmured the big man.

'But you're not suggesting that he was — was mixed up in this?' said Trainor in bewilderment.

'He was killed here,' broke in Mr. Budd. 'In the cellar below, where he had been kept prisoner. And he was killed by the same person who murdered Marsh, Krayle and Devine.'

'No, no! You're wrong. You must be wrong!' asserted Trainor with conviction, shaking his head. 'It's impossible! What could he have to do with it?'

'With what?' snapped the superintendent quickly. 'With what, Mr. Trainor?'

'With the murder of Marsh and the rest of it, of course,' said Trainor impatiently.

'Why is it impossible?' murmured Mr. Budd, relapsing into his habitual sleepy-eyed, lethargic manner. 'What has got to do with the murder of Marsh and the rest of it, Mr. Trainor?'

'The — ' Trainor closed his lips quickly and stopped abruptly.

'Go on, sir,' said the big man softly. 'The — what?'

'Nothing!' muttered the other. 'I'm not saying any more.'

'That's a pity — a great pity,' said Mr. Budd sorrowfully, 'because I believe what you was goin' to say might have been interestin'.' He turned towards the gaping Tipman, who had been listening attentively to this interchange. 'We'll have to get an expert down from London to open this,' he said, jerking his head towards the safe. 'But we can't do that until the morning, so we may as well shut the panel. I suppose if we reverse the openin' business it'll close.'

He climbed wearily up on to the chair again and tried. As he expected, the panel slid noisily up, covering the cavity.

'Now everythin's neat and tidy again,'

he remarked, getting down. 'Hammond here 'ull see that nothin's touched until the safe's opened. I think that's all we can do for the moment. I'll be gettin' back to the manor, and I think it 'ud be a good idea if you came with me, Mr. Trainor.'

Trainor hesitated, looked from one to the other, and then clearing his throat, he nodded. 'You — you really mean to have that safe opened tomorrow?' he asked a little huskily.

'I most certainly do, sir!' declared Mr. Budd. 'In my opinion, the sooner we find out what's inside the better.'

* * *

Although it had been after two before the superintendent had gone to bed, he was up and down early on the following morning, long before anyone else, with the exception of Pullman and Mary Hutton.

The discovery of the safe and his late return had necessitated an alteration in the arrangements he had previously made with Leek. Much to that melancholy man's relief, he had decided to postpone setting a watch until the following night. He concluded that, since the people in the house must be aware that someone had been up and wakeful until the early hours, the midnight prowler would not risk leaving his room. And apparently this conclusion was right, for nothing had happened to disturb the serenity of the household.

'You're up early, sir,' said the yellow-faced butler, meeting Mr. Budd in the hall, and his voice held a faint tinge of resentment.

'Early to bed and early to rise makes a man healthy, wealthy and wise,' said the big man sententiously. 'Not that I went to bed early, so maybe I'll only be healthy and wise.' He reached for his overcoat and struggled into it.

'You goin' out, sir?' enquired Pullman, a little surprised.

'I'm goin' to take a little exercise in the fresh mornin' air,' replied Mr. Budd gravely, and the butler eyed him curiously.

For a moment the superintendent thought he was on the point of asking where he was going, but if this had been in his mind he refrained from putting it into words.

'Perhaps you'd like a cup of tea, sir, before you go?' he suggested.

'Now that's an idea,' said Mr. Budd. 'I should very much like a cup of tea, Pullman.'

'Miss Hutton has just made some for ourselves,' said the butler. 'If you'll wait a moment, sir, I'll bring you a cup.'

He disappeared in the direction of the kitchen and the stout man went over to the front door, opened it, and peered out. It was not a pleasant morning. A drizzle of rain was falling and the sky was grey and cloudy. The promise of a crisp frost which the previous night had held out had not been fulfilled.

Pullman came back with a cup of tea which Mr. Budd gulped gratefully, and then pulling his muffler up to his chin he set forth.

Breakfast was over when he returned, and Sergeant Leek was lounging miserably about the hall. 'Where have you been?' asked that melancholy man as Mr.

173

Budd came in. 'I've been 'untin' for you everywhere.'

'Why?' demanded his superior as he slipped out of his wet coat. 'Anythin' happened?'

'No, nothin's 'appened,' said the sergeant, 'but I couldn't make out where you'd got to. You never said nothin' to me about goin' out.'

'That was very wrong of me,' said Mr. Budd. 'Where's Miss Marsh?'

'In there, talkin' to that lawyer feller.' Leek jerked his narrow head towards the door of the lounge.

'Anybody else with them?' asked the detective.

'No,' said the sergeant. 'The rest of 'em have cleared off to their rooms. Nice, sociable lot, I don't think!'

'Everybody knows that,' said the super-intendent rudely, and went into the lounge.

Cathleen and Rutherford were standing by the fire, talking in low tones, and they looked up as he entered.

'Good mornin', Miss Marsh,' he said. 'Good mornin', Mr. Rutherford. I'm glad I've caught you both alone, because I wanted to have a word with you — particularly with you, miss.'

'What is it?' asked the woman a little apprehensively.

'It's nothin' to worry about,' said Mr. Budd, 'but it's interestin' and peculiar. I've just been over to Seldon Magna makin' a few inquiries, and I've learned somethin' that seems to me a bit queer. Maybe you knew all about it?'

'About what?' asked Rutherford.

'Well, it appears,' said Mr. Budd, 'that Mr. Marsh, about twelve months before he died, bought a piece of property that belonged to Sir Alfred Mowbury.'

'A piece of property?' echoed the woman in a puzzled tone as he paused. 'What sort of property?'

'That's the queer bit,' replied the big man. 'You remember tellin' me about that ruined inn, the Witches' Moon?'

She stared at him in bewilderment and nodded.

'Well, that's the bit of property he bought,' said Mr. Budd. 'He bought the freehold of the Witches' Moon.'

'I knew nothing about it,' she said,

amazed. 'Did you, Mr. Rutherford?'

'Nothing at all!' the lawyer declared.

'I didn't suppose you did, either of you,' remarked Mr. Budd, 'because I'm given to understand that the deal was carried out with the utmost secrecy.'

'But what on earth could — could Father have wanted with that dilapidated old place?' muttered Cathleen. 'It's useless to anyone, even for rebuilding.'

'I don't think he wanted it for that purpose,' said the superintendent. 'I think maybe I could tell you what he wanted it for.'

He gave a brief account of his discoveries of the previous night.

'But there's nothing to show,' said Rutherford, 'that this safe belonged to Marsh.'

'I don't entirely agree with you, sir,' said Mr. Budd. 'It's a modern safe and it certainly wasn't there when he bought the property. There's no direct evidence, I'll admit, that it was Mr. Marsh's; but all the same I think we can pretty safely take it that it was, especially after Mr. Trainor's behaviour.'

'But,' said the lawyer in perplexity, 'why the deuce go to the expense of buying a place like that in order to install a safe? Why couldn't he have brought the safe here?'

'Ah, why couldn't he!' said Mr. Budd thoughtfully. 'Now I think you've hit on something, sir. You'd no knowledge that this safe was there?'

'I certainly hadn't!' declared Rutherford.

'Nor you, miss?'

'No,' she replied. 'I knew nothing about it, or I should have told you.'

'I guessed you didn't,' murmured the big man, 'but I just wanted to make sure. So this safe was a secret of your father's?'

'If it belonged to him — yes,' she admitted.

'In which case it hasn't been opened since he was killed,' he went on. 'Now, it's my opinion there's important evidence in it concernin' his death. The property now rightly belongs to you, includin', of course, the safe. Have we your permission to send for a man and have it opened?'

'Don't give your permission, Cathleen,' broke in a husky voice. 'Don't give it!'

They swung round and faced Alice Devine. She was standing in the doorway, her big, pasty face pale and lined, one hand pressed tightly to her breast. 'Don't give your permission!' she repeated. 'It is your property. They can do nothing unless you allow it.'

'If you'll excuse me, ma'am — ' began Mr. Budd, but she took no notice of him and went on as though he had not spoken.

'If you give your permission for that safe to be opened you'll regret it all your life!' she cried.

'But how can I refuse, Alice?' said the woman. 'There may be something — '

'Of course you can refuse!' broke in the woman impatiently.

'I think Alice is right, Cathleen.' Trainor's voice came from the hall. 'Don't let them open it. It can do no good.'

'How do you know it can do no good?' snapped Mr. Budd. 'D'you know what that safe contains, sir?'

'No,' said Trainor, appearing behind Alice Devine. 'But I think it's better left unopened.'

'It mustn't be opened!' said the

woman, catching her breath. 'It mustn't be opened, I tell you!'

'What are you all talking about?' exclaimed Cathleen. 'Why shouldn't the safe be opened?'

Alice Devine gave a loud, shrill laugh. 'Ask Gerald, ask your aunt, ask Leslie, ask Mr. Hope. I don't expect they'll tell you, but ask them.'

'We're askin' you at the moment, ma'am!' said Mr. Budd sternly. 'Why shouldn't Mr. Marsh's safe be opened?'

She turned on him like a fury. 'Why! Why!' she screamed. 'You're always asking questions. Nothing but questions! Can't you leave well alone? Hasn't enough harm been done already? Hebert Marsh is dead, and everything connected with his death was dead. It was over and done with, and now you want to stir it all up again! Why couldn't you leave it alone?'

'Because, ma'am,' said the superintendent, 'somebody was responsible for killin' Mr. Marsh, and justice has got to be done!'

'Oh, you fool! You fool!' she cried wildly. 'Justice was done! Marsh died because he wasn't fit to live! Don't you understand? *He wasn't fit to live!*' She screamed the words in a rising note that ended in a sob.

'She's hysterical!' said Rutherford sharply. 'Better get her back to her room.'

'What in the world's the row about? What's happening?' asked the lazy voice of Leslie Curtis as he came hurrying in. 'What the devil's the matter, Alice?'

But she didn't answer him. Her wild outburst had exhausted her and she clung to the back of a chair, sobbing jerkily.

'God knows what's the matter with her, Leslie,' said Cathleen. 'Or what's the matter with anyone else in this house! The police have discovered a hidden safe belonging to Father at the old inn. You know, the Witches' Moon — '

'A hidden safe?' Curtis interrupted her, and the lazy drawl had gone. His tone was sharp and hard and edgy.

'Yes,' interjected Trainor. 'And the police want permission to force it open. I've advised Cathleen to refuse.'

'You're right!' agreed the other promptly. 'Perfectly right! Don't let them open it,

180

Cathleen! It's much better not to, I assure you.'

'I'd very much like to know, sir,' said Mr. Budd, 'why you're all so certain that the openin' of this safe isn't goin' to do any good?' He looked round him sleepily, but they didn't answer. 'I should like to point out,' he went on, 'that if the police think it necessary, which they do, to have the safe opened, it can be done without anyone's permission.'

Still there was silence, broken only by the muffled sobbing from Alice Devine. Then Trainor let go his breath with a long sigh and shrugged his shoulders. 'Do what you like,' he said shortly, and thrust his hands into his pocket. 'Only don't forget — I warned you!' Without another word he turned on his heel and walked away. Cathleen looked after him, and then, with a hard face she turned to the big man.

'Do what you like,' she said. 'If you want to open the safe open it. You have my full permission.'

'Thank you, miss,' murmured Mr. Budd. 'Now come along, Alice,' said Miss

Marsh, and her voice was completely unsympathetic. 'You'd better pull yourself together and come to your room. Perhaps if you lie down for a little while you'll feel better.' She took the woman by the arm, and after a slight hesitation Alice Devine allowed herself to be led away.

'Well,' said Curtis, 'I suppose nothing I can say will alter your decision?'

'I'm afraid nothin' anyone can say will alter my decision,' murmured Mr. Budd. The other shrugged his shoulders.

'Very well,' he said. 'You heard what Trainor said? We've both warned you. If you open that safe you'll be sorry.'

'So, apparently, will a good many people,' said the superintendent. 'Why don't you want that safe opened, Mr. Curtis?'

'When you open it — if you ever do,' retorted Curtis unpleasantly, 'you'll know!'

9

The Warning

'What d'you make of it, Superintendent?' asked Rutherford, breaking a long silence.

Mr. Budd shrugged his shoulders irritably. 'I can't make head or tail of it,' he confessed. 'Except that they all know somethin' and that they're mighty keen that that safe shouldn't be opened.'

They were alone in the lounge, for Leslie Curtis, after his last remark, had abruptly left them.

'That's obvious,' said the lawyer. 'What are they afraid of?'

'What they was all afraid of before, sir,' said the big man. 'That somethin' 'ull come out which'll bring to light the truth concernin' these murders. That's what they're afraid of, and that's what they've *always* been afraid of.'

'But it's ridiculous to suppose,' said Rutherford, 'that they're *all* mixed up in it?'

'I don't think it's ridiculous at all,' disagreed Mr. Budd. 'In fact I'm willin' to bet they *are!*'

'Are you seriously suggesting that all these people are concerned in a murder conspiracy?' demanded the lawyer.

'Oh, no! I'm not goin' as far as that.' The superintendent shook his head. 'I don't think they know who killed Marsh and the others. But I'm pretty sure they know *why*, and the *why* affects them all equally.'

'Well, it's a queer business,' grunted Rutherford. 'I wish Miss Marsh had left it alone.'

'I think she wishes that now, too, sir,' said Mr. Budd. 'But it's just as well she didn't. Maybe it would have been worse if she had than it is now.'

'If she hadn't had this idea of inviting these people here,' said Rutherford, 'Krayle wouldn't be dead and Devine would still be alive. I don't see how it could have been worse.'

'Don't you, sir?' said the detective. 'Well, it's my opinion that there would have been trouble, anyway. And if it hadn't happened here it would have been worse, for this reason: if these people had been killed elsewhere, we shouldn't have had such a narrow field to look for the murderer.'

'That's true,' muttered the lawyer. 'Well, I hope you find him, and soon. I don't mind admitting that I shall be very glad when it's all over.'

'So shall I,' said Mr. Budd. 'It's a pretty big responsibility, because until I can find the killer nobody's safe.'

'Do you suspect anyone?' inquired Rutherford, unconsciously paraphrasing Inspector Tipman's question.

'Yes,' said the superintendent, to his surprise. 'I do. I suspect everybody. And I shall go on suspectin' 'em until I find the right one.'

Rutherford left him a few seconds later, and when he was alone Mr. Budd produced one of his black cigars, lit it with care, and puffed contentedly. The expert from London was due to arrive at twelve o'clock. He had arranged to meet him with Inspector Tipman at the Witches' Moon, and until then he could do nothing further.

What was there inside that steel box which, at the prospect of its being found, had filled the inmates of this house with alarm? Had they and Hebert Marsh been mixed up in some nefarious business that was against the law? Were they afraid that the safe contained evidence that would render them all liable to arrest and criminal proceedings? It seemed a far-fetched idea, and the detective, quite unconsciously, shook his head. There was no need for any of these people to enter into a criminal conspiracy. They were all rich. George Devine's yearly income from his plays and books must have run well into five figures, and Hebert Marsh, too, had spent money lavishly. The others, with the exception of Emily Marsh, were all well-off. It was queer where her money had gone. Maybe the inquiries he had initiated, and which were being carried out by a certain patient and diligent sergeant in London, would throw some light on this.

He went out into the kitchen to find Pullman, but the butler was not there.

Mary Hutton was peeling potatoes at the table and in reply to his question jerked her head towards the half-open door leading into the scullery. 'He's outside, chopping wood,' she said; and then, as Mr. Budd was crossing to the door: 'Is that right — about the safe?'

He stopped and looked at her keenly. 'What do you know about it?' he asked.

'I don't know nothin' about it,' she answered hurriedly. 'I only heard you all talkin'.' She seemed on the point of saying something more, for her lips parted, but she closed them again as though she had thought better of it.

The big man's eyes narrowed to slits. Even this woman, with the untidy mop of grey hair which straggled over her face, knew something; was hiding something. Her question had been a little too eager, her denial too hurried to be quite natural. As he watched her he saw that his gaze was making her feel nervous, for a potato slipped from her fingers and splashed into the pan of water from which she had taken it. In spite of all her efforts, her fingers were shaking.

'What are you afraid of?' he asked sharply, and she looked up.

'I've cause to be afraid, haven't I?' she answered. 'Two people killed in the last few days. Ain't that enough to frighten anyone?' She laid down her knife and leaned forward. 'Get 'em all away from here,' she said. 'Leave the place empty and deserted as it was, and there'll be no more trouble. There's somethin' 'ere that doesn't like company. Somethin' that 'ud rather be alone!'

'Do you mean a ghost?' he asked, and there was no levity in his voice.

'You can call it what you like,' answered the woman. 'I ain't givin' it no names. Whatever it was it came three years ago and it's been 'ere ever since, and all the police in the world won't drive it away!'

She refused to say anything more, and he went out into the weed-choked yard to find Pullman. He was not chopping wood and there was no sign that he had been. He was talking to Lionel Hope, and they both looked round, startled, when the detective appeared.

'Good morning, Superintendent,' said

the small, meek little man a trifle nervously. 'I hear that you — you've made a discovery at an old ruin in the district?'

'Everybody seems to have heard that,' remarked Mr. Budd. 'You're quite right, sir; I've found a safe which I've every reason to believe belonged to Mr. Marsh. Can you tell me anythin' about it?'

'Me?' Hope licked his lips and shook his bald head. 'No. How should I know anything about it?'

'I was wonderin',' said the big man. 'It's a curious thing, but everybody keeps on talkin' about it, and yet nobody seems to know anythin'. Did you know that Mr. Marsh owned the Witches' Moon?'

Pullman, to whom the question had been addressed, stared at him blankly. 'No,' he said after a pause, 'I didn't know nothin', sir.' Yet his face had gone paler, and there was fear in his watery blue eyes.

'Well, we're goin' to open it this mornin',' said Mr. Budd, 'and I've got an idea we shall find a lot that's very interestin'.'

'You know your own business best, of course, Superintendent,' muttered Hope, 'but I really think — I'm inclined to believe that perhaps it would be wiser to — to leave well alone.'

'You'd be surprised,' said the Superintendent, 'what a lot of people agree with you. But I don't happen to be one of them.'

He left them, curious to know what they had been talking about when he had interrupted their low-voiced conversation.

It was a quarter past eleven when he left the house, and he reached The Witches' Moon at twenty minutes to twelve. Hammond was no longer on duty, but his place has been taken by another constable, a big red-faced man, stolid and bucolic. Mr. Budd concluded that this was Wullen, Hammond's relief.

The constable had nothing to report. Nobody had been near the inn. He was chatting to the man when Inspector Tipman arrived. He was accompanied by a small, alert man with a bird-like face who carried a large and apparently heavy bag. The inspector introduced him as Mr. May, and explained that he was from a safe manufacturer's in London.

He deposited his bag on the floor of the bar parlour and they showed him the safe. He surveyed it with a gloomy look and nodded his small head. 'It should only take about 'alf an hour,' he said in a melancholy voice, the first words he had spoken, and proceeded to unpack his bag. It contained a variety of queer-looking objects, chief among which was a small box that resembled a portable wireless. A pair of earphones, attached to a long flex, was plugged into this, and the interested Mr. Budd learned that it was the amplifier which magnified the sound of the falling tumblers and enabled the miserable-looking Mr. May to discover the combination.

Methodically the safe expert laid out his instruments, switched on a powerful hand electric lamp, and examined the face of the safe. He had only spoken eight words since he had arrived, and apparently had no intention of speaking again.

Carefully he adjusted the headphones and pressed the rubber ring of a small microphone against the steel door of the safe in the vicinity of the dial. His hand was on the knob when there came the sound of hurried footsteps, and a sharp cry filled the little room. Swinging round, Mr. Budd saw the figure of Emily Marsh standing in the open doorway of the bar parlour, with Rutherford and Cathleen behind her.

'Stop!' she cried shrilly. 'Stop! You don't know what you're doing. It's death to open that safe!'

'Aunt Emily, come back!' Cathleen laid a hand on her arm.

'I won't come back!' cried the woman. 'They must not open that safe. It's death to touch it!' She glared at Mr. Budd and Inspector Tipman, and the big man took a step towards her.

'I'm sorry, ma'am,' he said soothingly, 'if it should upset you, but the safe has got to be opened.'

She regarded him steadily, and her thin lips curled in a sneer. 'You can open it — if you can find the combination,' she answered in a hard voice. 'Otherwise I warn you to leave it alone! My brother told me about it, and I assure you if you attempt to force it, it means death!'

'What d'you mean, ma'am?' asked Mr. Budd. 'We havent' got any time to — '

'I mean,' said the old woman, 'that my brother knew how to protect his property. He had explosives fixed in that safe so that nobody could tamper with it who didn't know the right combination!'

'Good Lord!' muttered Tipman, his jaw dropping. 'Explosives! D'you think she's speaking the truth?'

Emily Marsh's ears were sensitive. She turned her smouldering eyes on him. 'Try, if you don't believe me!' she almost screamed. 'Try! And you'll be blown to pieces. Go on — open the safe now — if you dare!'

*   *   *

Mr. Budd took the stump of the cigar, which had gone out, from between his lips, and threw it irritably into the fireplace. He was both annoyed and nonplussed.

He stood at the window of the room which had been allotted to him at Wildcroft Manor and stared moodily out at the uninspiring greyness of the afternoon. He had hoped for great things from the opening of the safe, and Emily Marsh's dramatic appearance had effectually shattered his hopes.

Whether she had been speaking the truth or not it was impossible to say, but the taciturn Mr. May had stolidly refused to take the risk, and the big man could not altogether blame him. It was sufficiently possible to prohibit any foolhardy experiments, and so the safe expert gathered up his paraphernalia and departed, leaving the safe unopened. It was galling and exasperating, but there was no help for it.

Mr. Budd pursed his lips and frowned. He was more convinced than ever that the secret of Hebert Marsh's death was to be found in that carefully guarded repository at the old inn. The relief on the faces of everyone concerned when they heard that the opening had been abandoned was sufficient confirmation, if he had needed any.

To add to his ill humour, there had been no report from London concerning the inquiries he had set on foot regarding Krayle. The dead man's flat had been thoroughly searched, but no paper or document referring to the safe deposit mentioned in Devine's letter had been discovered. Nor had inquiries at banks and strong-rooms yielded any better result. At Krayle's own bank he had deposited nothing in the nature of documents, and his name was unknown at any of the possible repositories for such things. Either Devine had been mistaken, or Krayle had rented such a safe in a false name.

The possibility that the safe referred to was the one at the Witches' Moon had crossed the superintendent's mind, but he dismissed it instantly. That safe had been known to no one except Hebert Marsh, and he had taken extraordinary precautions to ensure that it could not be opened except by himself. Neither Rutherford nor Cathleen had been aware of its existence, or knew the combination which would gain access to its contents.

It was a queer business, and the further you went the queerer it became.

Why had Marsh kept that safe in such an inaccessible place? Why hadn't he installed it in his own house, instead of going to the expense of buying a derelict ruin to house it?

The carving, and the secret compartment in which it stood, had not been made especially. They were old — as ancient as the ramshackle building itself. Probably Marsh had discovered the existence of that hidden cupboard, and his discovery had suggested the use to which he had put it. And he had bought the safe from the firm for whom James Augustus Dench had worked. That seemed pretty obvious. But had he brought it to the Witches' Moon himself, or had Dench fixed it for him?

Mr. Budd was inclined to think that he had brought it himself. After taking so much trouble to ensure secrecy, it was hardly likely that he would have taken anybody into his confidence.

But what was the object?

He turned away from the window despondently and sat down on the edge of the bed. What the rest of the household were doing he neither knew nor cared. So long as none of them attempted to leave, he was not particularly interested.

He fished out a fresh cigar from his waistcoat pocket and lit it, smoking thoughtfully. If only there had been a photograph of Krayle in existence . . .

He stiffened, and the sleepy look that was habitual with him changed to a momentary alertness. Ten minutes later he was on his way to the police station at Mallington to put the idea, which had come to him so suddenly, into execution.

★ ★ ★

Police-Constable Hammond took a bulky package from his pocket and carefully unwrapped it. From the grease-proof paper he produced half a loaf and a large wedge of cheese. Putting these on a cracked plate, which he had found, he turned his attention to the singing kettle on the old range. It was boiling, and he poured the water carefully into the teapot which stood warming on the stove. When the tea was brewed, he carried it over to the table and set it beside the milk and sugar which he had brought with him.

Taking off his tunic he poured out a cup of tea, and, sitting down, began to munch the bread and cheese slowly.

This was his supper, and it made a welcome break in the monotony of his job. He had little relish for his task, although it was better than patrolling a beat in the thin drizzle which was falling outside. The old building, with its eerie reputation and its queer noises, got on his nerves, and made him start at the slightest sound. It was not reassuring, either, to know that that safe was full of explosives which might go up at any moment. All things considered, Hammond decided that he would be very glad indeed when his job was over.

He finished his supper, piled the dirty things neatly together, and pouring out a second cup of tea, produced from the pocket of his tunic several football coupons. With a frowning brow, he proceeded to make his selections for the week. He was a staunch supporter of Mr. Littlewood, and indulged in rosy dreams of colossal dividends which would enable him to resign from the force and live a subsequent life of leisure. Contrary to all the rules and regulations, he also regaled himself with a cigarette.

It was very still and silent, except for the drip-drip of the rain and the occasional cracking of the old woodwork — sounds to which he had, more or less, grown accustomed; and with great deliberation and much thought, he completed the filling-in of his coupon and studied it reflectively. Perhaps he would be lucky this time. He sat back in his chair and allowed his mind to weave pictures of what he would do if he were.

Either the warmth of the kitchen, his supper, or both, presently caused him to nod. His chin dropped onto his breast, and sleep so dulled his senses that he failed to hear the new sound which had imposed itself upon the drippings of the water from the leaky roof. It was faint and barely audible — a gentle creaking — and it came from the dark void beyond the half-closed door of the kitchen. It ceased, and a rumbling snore emanated from the sleeping constable. The door moved slowly and the dim figure of a man appeared on the threshold.

He peered at the sleeping policeman, and smiled beneath the handkerchief that concealed the lower part of his face. Noiselessly he slid from his pocket a short length of hard rubber, and tiptoed forward until he was immediately behind the unsuspecting sleeper. His gloved hand grasping the cosh rose and fell. The crescendo cadence of a snore was cut short as the constable slumped sideways in his chair and rolled to the floor.

The man with the cosh stooped, examined the sprawling figure, and then, straightening up, pocketed his weapon and hurried over to the door. Moving into the darkness of the passage, he pulled a torch from his pocket and switched it on. Making his way to the main entrance, he fumbled with the fastenings, opened the door, and whistled softly. Out of the wet night loomed a second man.

'Everything O.K.?' he whispered.

'Yes,' said the first man with a nod, 'he'll be quiet enough for a few minutes — time enough for what we've got to do anyway.' He motioned the newcomer inside and closed the door. 'Come on,' he continued. 'This way.' He led the way to the bar-parlour, entered, and swept his light over the carving. 'Once right, twice left,' he muttered. 'Get me that chair.'

His companion brought it in silence, and the other mounted. Gripping the moon, he twisted it as Mr. Budd had done, and with the same result. The panel dropped, disclosing the safe. Getting hurriedly down, the first man joined the other and they both peered into the opening.

'It isn't fixed,' said the man with the torch, flashing the light on the steel door, 'so it shouldn't be difficult to shift. Give me a hand and let's try.'

'I s'pose it's all right,' grunted his companion doubtfully. 'Them explosives won't go off, will they?'

'Of course it's all right, you fool!' snarled the first man. 'They only act if anyone tries to force the thing.'

''Ow d'yer know that?' was the quick retort. 'I wouldn't be too sure if I was you — '

'I tell you I am sure!' snapped the other. 'It's quite safe unless it's dropped.

It might blow up then, of course. Now come on, otherwise that damned policeman may come round.' He set his torch down on the chair so as to have both hands free, and reaching into the cupboard-like compartment grasped one side of the safe.

'Come on,' he said impatiently as the other held back. 'There's nothing to be afraid of. I don't suppose it's very heavy, and we've only got to carry it to the car — '

'Leave it where it is, if you please!' droned a sleepy voice gently. 'An' put up your hands. I'm not what you might call a dead shot, but I don't think I could very well miss doin' a certain amount of damage at such close range!'

Startled, the two men swung round. They had heard no sound, but in the doorway lounged the figure of Mr. Budd, whose right hand was clasped round the butt of a very business-like automatic.

10

Mr. Budd Is Not Pleased

'Go on, do as you're told,' drawled the stout man. 'I don't hold with procrastination.' He made a gesture with the barrel of the pistol, and the smaller of the two men raised his arms. 'Now you,' ordered Mr. Budd, and the other started to obey, but as his hands slowly rose above his head he suddenly kicked out at the chair on which the torch rested. It went over with a crash and the light went out!

The move had been so unexpected that the big man was taken unawares. His finger tightened on the trigger of the pistol and it exploded with a loud report, but before he could fire again there was a rush of feet in the darkness; he was hurled violently against the jamb of the door, lost his balance, and fell heavily. His elbow struck the floor and a numbing pain shot up his arm. The automatic dropped from his nerveless fingers and went clattering across the bare boards as the door of the old inn closed with a loud bang.

Breathlessly Mr. Budd scrambled to his feet, rubbing his injured arm. It was useless attempting to follow the men. The car in which they had come was already moving off, and by the time he reached the road it would be gone. He listened to the fading sound of the engine with mixed feelings. He had bungled it badly. He had been within an ace of solving the whole problem, and he had let the chance slip through his fingers.

It had been a mistake to come inside the inn at all. He should have waited by the car — or better still, in the car. He would have caught them that way. Well, it was no use bothering *now*. The harm was done. The men, whoever they were, had got away, and all he had to console him was the fact that they had got away empty-handed. That, and the number of the car. It was something, anyway, though he didn't feel very optimistic about the usefulness of the number. He felt very doubtful if it would lead to any worthwhile discovery.

While these thoughts were running through his mind, he was groping about in the darkness in search of the torch, and after a little while he found it. But it was useless. The fall must have damaged the bulb, for it refused to light.

Mr. Budd swore gently. He had no matches — the last had been used to light a cigar on the way up to the old inn.

As he stumbled towards the door he heard a muffled groan, and remembered the constable who should have been on guard. The groan sounded as though the man had been injured, and Mr. Budd hurried as quickly as he could toward the kitchen from whence the sound had come. A light shone through the partly open door, and pushing the door wide the big man looked in.

The constable was sitting up on the floor, clutching at his head; and going over, Mr. Budd knelt beside him. 'Take it easy,' he said kindly. 'What did they do, cosh you?'

The man nodded and groaned again.

'Took you by surprise, I suppose,' said

Mr. Budd, passing one hand rapidly over the policeman's skull. 'Well, they don't appear to have done any serious damage. Keep quiet and you'll be all right in a minute or two.'

He went out into the scullery and fetched some water in the cup, which the constable drank greedily; and then, with the assistance of the big man, he got gingerly to his feet. 'Gosh! My 'ead don't 'alf 'urt,' he muttered.

'I expect it does,' said Mr. Budd, 'but you're lucky to be able to feel anythin'. What happened, exactly?'

With many pauses, the injured Hammond told him. 'God knows 'oo 'e was, or what 'e was after, sir,' he concluded. 'If it was an 'e,' he added.

'It was a 'he' all right,' said Mr. Budd. 'In fact it was two 'he's.'

'Did you see 'em, sir?' asked the dazed policeman.

'I did,' Mr. Budd said with a nod. 'And I felt 'em, too!' He rubbed his still-tingling arm. 'I wish I'd caught 'em, but anyhow, I was in time to stop 'em clearin' off with that safe.'

'Was that wot they was after?' said the constable, opening his bloodshot eyes wide.

'Yes,' answered Mr. Budd. 'An' I'm very glad they didn't get it. I don't s'pose they'll try again tonight, but I'll have a double guard put on all the same. How do you feel? Think you can carry on until I can send someone along to relieve you?'

'Yes, sir,' said Hammond. 'I'll be quite all right in a bit.'

'You'd better get along home to bed as soon as you can, though,' said the stout man. 'I'll have two men up here to take your place inside an hour, an' then you just clear off an' 'ave a good sleep. That'll put you right. In the meanwhile there's a loaded pistol of mine in the bar-parlour. Hang on to that while I'm gone, an' don't be afraid to use it if anybody you don't know tries to get in.'

He took his departure, leaving the constable sitting grimly by the table with the pistol gripped firmly in his hand, an expression of watchful determination on his solid face.

It was after midnight when the

superintendent entered the police station at Mallington; and he found, as he had expected, that Inspector Tipman had long since gone home. A message, however, brought him post-haste, half dressed and sleepy-eyed. He listened in astonishment to what Mr. Budd had to say, and instantly despatched two men to relieve the injured Hammond. 'What took you up to the inn so late?' he asked curiously, when this had been attended to.

'Insomnia,' replied Mr. Budd untruthfully. 'I was walkin' past the place when I saw the car, and knew somethin' was up.'

He did not think it was necessary to explain to the inspector that he had felt suddenly uneasy, and that it was pure chance that had taken him in the direction of the Witches' Moon, the almost unconscious prompting of an inner voice that whispered all was not well. Tipman would not have understood, and Mr. Budd was rather sensitive about these hunches that sometimes came to him and had contributed in a large measure to his success.

'It's a pity you didn't catch those

fellers,' said the inspector, shaking his head. 'We might have learned a lot if you had.'

'I think we should,' grunted the big man, 'but I didn't, so there you are. Maybe the car can be traced; you've got the number.'

It was, but it did not help them very much. It was found abandoned in the early hours of that morning on the outskirts of a wood fifteen miles away, and subsequent inquiries elicited the fact that it had been stolen from a car park in a neighbouring town.

The inquest had been fixed for ten o'clock, and Mr. Budd, looking even more sleepy than usual, arrived at the little schoolhouse in Kings Mailing, where the proceedings were due to take place punctually. Nothing very sensational was likely to accrue from the inquiry, for the superintendent had arranged with Tipman that it was to be as short and as formal as possible. Evidence of identification and the medical testimony would be taken, and then the police would ask for an adjournment.

There were plenty of people crowding in and around the temporary court, among whom Mr. Budd noticed several reporters. They noticed him and tried to corner him, but he managed to dodge them.

The coroner, a fussy little man with a great air of importance, arrived, and the jury were sworn in. When they had returned from viewing the body, the coroner coughed, rustled his papers, and began his preliminary address. It was quite brief, and the proceedings which followed were, as Mr. Budd had expected, without incident, until the name of Gerald Trainor was called, and then it was discovered that Gerald Trainor was not there. Neither did anyone appear to know what had become of him.

None of the people from Wildcroft Manor had seen him that morning. He had not had breakfast with the rest, and they concluded that he was late getting up. Mr. Budd had not noticed his absence before. He had not come to the inquest with the others, and he had had his breakfast before they were up in order to see Leek off to London by the early train from Mallington.

'This is very annoying,' said the coroner testily. 'The man must be found. He's an important witness.'

'Probably he is still at the house, sir,' said Tipman with a worried frown. 'I'll send somebody to see.'

He did, but Gerald Trainor was not at the house. He was not anywhere. Sometime during the darkness of the night he had disappeared.

The inquest proceeded without Gerald Trainor, and after the formal evidence of death had been taken, was adjourned for a fortnight. The fussy little coroner was inclined to be annoyed, for he had obviously been looking forward to a protracted inquiry, but he consented to Tipman's request after some hesitation.

The absence of Trainor seemed to have a peculiar effect on the others. Mrs. Devine, looking pale and ill, kept glancing uneasily at Leslie Curtis and Lionel Hope. Cathleen's face was expressionless, but there was a queer, hurt look in her eyes, and something else that Mr. Budd could not quite place.

Of the little community which had started as ten, only seven now remained. Krayle and Devine were dead, and Trainor was — where? Had he gone away of his own free will, or was he, too, beyond the reach of all worries? Or — the thought crept into the big man's mind — was he the killer whose nerve had failed him at the last moment? Had Trainor been one of those men at the old inn, and had he been afraid that Mr. Budd had recognised him? The superintendent frowned, and his lips thinned. Questions, questions — without answers. That was the chief characteristic of this extraordinary affair.

Towards the afternoon, however, one fact came to light. Inspector Tipman came back from initiating inquiries to say that a man answering to Trainor's description had caught the first train that morning from Craysham, a small town twenty miles away. He had arrived on a bicycle, and had taken a single ticket for London. He had left the bicycle in the cloakroom, and this was the reason he had been remembered. A question to Pullman elicited the further fact that there had been an old bicycle belonging to Hebert Marsh in the outhouse. When they went to look for this they found that the lock had been smashed and the bicycle gone. Later the machine was identified by Cathleen as the one which had belonged to her father.

Mr. Budd telephoned to Scotland Yard, and inquiries were made at the terminus, but here all trace of Trainor was lost. There had been too many people on that train for the collector to remember any particular individual. 'An' it's goin' to be very difficult to pick him up,' remarked Mr. Budd sorrowfully. 'If he's clever, it's a thousand to one against his bein' found.'

Tipman nodded gloomily. 'You're right,' he said. 'He's given us the slip properly.'

But he was wrong, and so was Mr. Budd; for Gerald Trainor was to be found before the morning, in circumstances that neither of them had even imagined.

* * *

The policeman on patrol duty in Brinstone Square thought the night was cold, which indeed it was, and slapped his arms across his chest in order to rouse his sluggish circulation. A cutting wind had come up and was blowing from the east in fitful gusts that felt as though they were composed of all the disused razor-blades since these had been in existence. They stung and cut Constable Dawlish's ears until they glowed crimson. However, it was nearly the hour for his relief, and he consoled himself with visions of a hot supper and steaming coffee when he reached his little house at Brixton, and continued his soft-footed, majestic patrol of the big square.

He passed number thirty-seven on the corner, giving it more than a casual glance — for its owners were out of town, and he had received instructions to this effect — found nothing wrong with its outward appearance, and passed on his slow way. A clock somewhere in the distance chimed the hour of three as he turned the corner, and for five minutes afterwards the square was deserted. And then, out of the darkness of the night — for Brinstone Square is economically lighted — came the figure of a man.

He came from the direction of Piccadilly, walking briskly like a late reveller anxious to reach home. But this illusion was shattered when he drew level with the dark bulk of number thirty-seven, for here he halted abruptly, looked quickly about him, and then, climbing over the locked area gate, dropped into the little stone-paved court below.

The windows which gave light to the lower regions of the house were not protected by iron bars; and the man, after a moment's pause to assure himself that his action had not been seen, took a handkerchief from his pocket, wrapped it round his hand, and gave the glass just below the catch of one of the windows a sharp rap.

There was a little tinkling crash as the window broke, and thrusting his hand through the jagged aperture, he pushed back the hasp and gently raised the sash. A moment later he was inside and softly lowering the window. The whole episode had barely taken two minutes, and except for the broken pane — which could scarcely be seen from the pavement — there was nothing to show that an unlawful person had gained admittance to the shuttered house.

The intruder waited for a moment, his head on one side listening, but no sound greeted his ears, and presently he made his way cautiously across the big kitchen to a door on the opposite side. It was ajar, and pushing it open, he found himself in a dark passage. Closing the kitchen door so that no light could reach the windows, he took out a torch and flashed it on.

At the end of the passage a narrow flight of stairs led upwards to a door at the top. Mounting them, the man tried the handle and muttered an oath under his breath when he found that it was locked.

From the breast pocket of his overcoat he took a large chisel, and forcing it between the jamb, threw his weight on the handle. At the second attempt the door flew open with a sharp crack that sounded like a gun-shot in the silence.

216

Putting the chisel back in his pocket, the man stepped through into a big, gloomy hall and stood listening. He felt that that thunderous crash must have been heard all over the square, but apparently his fears were groundless, for no sound broke the stillness.

After a little while he moved forward until he came to the foot of the staircase. Pausing here again, he flashed his light up the dark well, and then began to ascend slowly. Presently he found himself on a wide landing from which several doors opened. He seemed to know the layout of the house well, for he ignored the two on the right, and made straight for the second door on the left. It was locked, as he had expected it would be, and again he had recourse to his chisel. When he had succeeded in forcing the door he entered a large, lofty room lined with books, evidently a library or study.

Switching out his torch, he made his way across to the big windows and carefully drew the heavy curtains. It would never do for his light to be seen from the square outside. When he had taken this precaution he switched on his light again and sent the ray dancing over the room. There was a big writing-table in the centre, but its surface was bare except for a blotting-pad, a silver inkstand, and a calendar. The intruder frowned thoughtfully. Where was the most likely place to find the thing he had come to seek?

He approached the writing-table and tried the drawers. There were five, two on each side and one in the middle. The two on either side opened at his touch, but they contained nothing except paper and envelopes — two of them in fact were practically empty.

He tried the centre drawer. It was locked. A swift wrench, however, disposed of the flimsy catch; and, pulling it open, he searched eagerly among the miscellaneous contents. But what he was looking for was not there.

Was it anywhere? This enterprise of his was almost a forlorn hope, but there was just a chance he might find it. If it was anywhere it would be in this room — the room where the dead owner of the house had spent most of his time. He stood rubbing his chin and glancing about him.

The furniture was still in the old position. Nothing had been moved. His eyes lighted on a cabinet in one corner, and he crossed over to it. It was of carved oak, and contained a nest of drawers. They were none of them locked, and he searched them rapidly but without result.

His quest had been fruitless. He tried every possible place but without finding what he sought, and an hour later he descended the stairs again and made his way to the kitchen. Raising the window through which he had entered, he slipped out into the area.

He was in the act of re-closing the window when a hand gripped his shoulder, and a voice said gruffly:

'Now then, young fellow-me-lad, you'll come on a little walk with me!'

With a gasp of alarm the burglar swung round and glared up into the face of Police-Constable Dawlish.

11

The Finding of Trainor

The desk-sergeant at Carlboro' police station laid down his pen and looked across at the constable who was standing in front of the fireplace. 'Business ain't what it used to be,' he remarked, shaking his grey head sorrowfully. 'Not since they closed them nightclubs. Why, I can remember when we was always busy, an' I was takin' down the charges as 'ard as I could go. No — ' He shook his head again. ' — things ain't what they was. Look at ternight. Nearly four o'clock, an' not even a drunk an' disorderly! Makes yer lose faith in 'uman nature!'

The constable, who had heard all this before, said nothing, and the sergeant continued: 'An' then there's all these 'ere rules an' regulations. Look at them! Spoilin' the business, that's what they are. If yer find a feller standin' over a dead body with a gun in 'is 'and, yer mustn't ask 'im what 'e's doin' or where 'e got 'is gun. Yer mus'n't ask 'im anything that'll make 'im incrim'nate 'isself.' He snorted. 'It's all wrong. Give me the good old-fashioned methods. Wot's the good o' treating 'em as if they was 'uman bein's? Crooks ain't 'uman, an' when yer start coddlin' 'em they don't understand it, they just takes advantage.'

'I suppose even crooks are entitled to fair play?' suggested the constable. He was a young man, and had had a university education, which had been of such amazing usefulness that he had been unable to obtain any kind of job, and had drifted into the Metropolitan Police Force.

'Fair play?' snarled the grizzled sergeant. 'They always *got* fair play! This ain't fair play, this is givin' 'em cream with their jam! An' wot about the people they rob an' murder? Ain't they entitled to fair play, too? Wot about all these undiscovered murderers durin' the last few years? Undiscovered!' He laughed scornfully. 'Why, in most cases we knows who did 'em, but we can't prove it because our 'ands is tied. We mustn't do this an' we mustn't do that, an' the cons'quence is that people go about killin' an' robbin' other people, and laughin' up their sleeves.

'Before all these new rules was made that couldn't 'ave 'appened. Mr. Jones was found dead, an' Mr. Smith, 'is nephew, wot was the heir to the will, was discovered to 'ave bloodstains on 'is coat. Before all this newfangled rubbish, Smith was pinched an' questioned as to how 'e came by them bloodstains. But yer can't do that now! He might tell yer that they came from the dead man's wound, and so incrim'nate 'isself!'

He stopped and looked towards the door as there came the measured tramp of feet from the street. 'Somethin's 'appened, any 'ow,' he said with satisfaction. 'One of our feller's 'as collared somebody by the sound of it.'

The door of the charge-room was pushed open and Police-Constable Dawlish entered importantly, gripping a tall, thin man by the arm. He marched him up to the sergeant's desk.

'At three forty-two I was on duty in Brinstone Square, when I saw this man climbing out of a window into the area of number thirty-seven,' he said in the curious monotone which policemen always use on such occasions. 'He refused to give his name, and I took him into custody . . .'

The sergeant picked up his pen and surveyed the prisoner sternly. 'Name?' he demanded briefly.

'Look here,' said the man, 'there's been a mistake. I'm a friend of the people who live at thirty-seven . . .'

'Long-lost son from Canada, maybe?' suggested the sergeant sarcastically. 'Come back to the family mansion after makin' a fortune. I've 'eard that tale before.'

'Look here . . .' began the other again.

'I'm lookin',' broke in the sergeant. 'An' I'm lookin' at a common burglar charged with breakin' an' enterin'. Now then, what's your name?'

The man regarded him for a moment in silence, and then shrugged his shoulders. 'Trainor,' he answered sullenly. 'Gerald Trainor.'

The sergeant held the pen poised over

the charge-sheet and raised his thick eyebrows. 'Oh, yer are, are yer?' he said. 'Then you're the feller we're all lookin' for. Connected with that business at Mallington, aren't yer? Skipped durin' the night.' He nodded several times. 'Here, Dawlish, fan 'im.'

The constable came over to his prisoner and scientifically went through his pockets. The contents were heaped on the sergeant's desk, and that worthy man made an inventory. He looked thoughtfully at the long-bladed chisel.

'I s'pose as you was a friend of the family you was bringing them this as a little keepsake?' he remarked. 'Or maybe carpentry's a hobby of yours?' He jerked his head toward the inner door as he picked up the telephone. 'Put him in the cooler,' he said shortly, and as Trainor was led away: 'Give me White' all 1212.'

A few seconds later he was speaking earnestly to an interested official at Scotland Yard.

★　★　★

The arrival of Inspector Tipman at Wildcroft Manor was at such an early hour that nobody was up. His continued battering on the knocker, however, at last brought a sleepy-eyed Pullman to see who was disturbing the peace.

'I want to see Superintendent Budd at once,' explained the inspector. 'It's very urgent.'

The servant went away grumbling, and presently the big man came down, rubbing his eyes. 'What's the idea of comin' here in the middle of the night?' he demanded irritably. 'I didn't get much sleep last night, an' now you go an' spoil what little I was . . . '

'Trainor has been found!' interrupted Tipman. 'I've just had a telephone message from the Yard.'

Mr. Budd was instantly wide awake. 'Where did they find him?' he asked.

'He was arrested in the area of the Marsh's town house,' said the inspector. 'He had forced an entry by breaking the kitchen window. They're detaining him at Carlboro' Police Station.'

'Broke into the Marsh's house, did he?'

the big man remarked. 'H'm, that's very interestin'. I think I'll get dressed an' go along an' see this feller Trainor.'

It was a quarter to seven when he brought his dingy little car to a halt outside Carlboro' Street Police Station. Getting laboriously down from behind the wheel, he entered the charge-room.

The desk-sergeant greeted him with a smile, for they were old friends. 'Come to see exhibit 'A', sir?' he asked cheerfully. 'I've been expectin' you. They told me at the Yard that you was on the case.'

'Has he made any statement?' inquired Mr. Budd, and the sergeant shook his head. ''E ain't said nuthin',' he replied. 'I've never come across a less talkative feller in me life.'

'I'll see him,' said the big man, yawning. 'Maybe he'll talk to me.'

The sergeant signalled to a constable, and Mr. Budd was led through a door at the back of the charge-room, along a bleak corridor, and down a flight of stone steps to the cells.

Trainor was sitting on the plank bed biting his nails when they entered, and he looked up with a sullen expression. 'Oh, it's you, is it?' he muttered ungraciously as he recognised the stout man. 'What do you want?'

'I want to ask you a few questions,' replied Mr. Budd, 'an' if you're a sensible man you'll answer 'em.'

'You can go to hell!' growled Trainor. 'I'll answer nothing.'

'You'll answer a charge of burglary if you're not careful,' retorted Mr. Budd. 'And maybe somethin' worse!'

The other's already pale face went a shade paler, but he said nothing.

'Now take my advice, an' don't be foolish,' went on the superintendent. 'Tell me why you took the risk of breakin' into Marsh's house this mornin'?'

'Because I wanted something,' grunted Trainor.

'I rather guessed that,' said Mr. Budd. 'An' I think I might try another guess an' tell you what it was.'

'If you know, why ask?' snarled Trainor disagreeably.

'Because I'd rather you told me,' answered the big man. 'You was lookin' for the combination that opens that safe, weren't you?'

Trainor looked at him steadily, but made no reply.

'Weren't you?' repeated Mr. Budd.

'If you must know, I was,' snapped the other. 'Now are you satisfied?'

'Not quite,' murmured Mr. Budd, shaking his head. 'Did you find it?'

'No.' This time there was no hesitation.

'Why were you so anxious to find it,' continued the superintendent, 'that you took the risk you did?'

'Because there is something in that safe that belongs to me,' answered Trainor.

'What?'

'That's my business,' said the other shortly. 'I've said all I'm going to say.'

Mr. Budd took out one of his black cigars and sniffed at it. 'Mr. Trainor,' he said at length, very softly, 'what hold had Hebert Marsh over you?'

The words were quietly spoken, but their effect on the man was electric. He sprang to his feet, his face grey and haggard. 'What do you mean?' he stammered. 'What do you mean?'

'I should've thought I spoke plainly enough,' said Mr. Budd, eyeing the startled man through half-closed lids. 'Marsh had some hold over you, didn't he? What was it?'

Trainor dropped back onto the bed, and every vestige of expression left his face. 'What makes you suppose that?' he asked harshly.

'Lots of things. An' puttin' two an' two together an' makin' 'em add up to four. I'm right, aren't I?'

'That's for you to find out,' said Trainor stubbornly. 'I'm not saying anything one way or the other.'

He stuck to this attitude in spite of all Mr. Budd's endeavours to persuade him to talk.

'You're a very foolish man, Mr. Trainor,' said the superintendent with a sigh as he prepared to take his leave. 'A very foolish man indeed. You might save a lot of trouble by tellin' me the truth, because I shall find it out for meself sooner or later.'

'That's your job,' retorted Trainor. 'Why should I do it for you?' And on this unsatisfactory note the interview ended.

Mr. Budd drove slowly to Scotland Yard, a frown on his heavy face, and his mind occupied with what he had just learned. For he had learned something. Trainor's refusal to talk had been as good as an admission. When he had suggested that Marsh had had some hold on the man, it had been more or less a shot in the dark. But Trainor's reaction to the question had proved just how right he had been. Here, through all the darkness, was the first faint glimmer of light; and it could, with a little coaxing, be turned into a glaring illumination. There was not much doubt in which direction the dim ray was pointing. Blackmail! That was it. And if that *was* it, then it explained a lot. The queer behaviour of all those people at Wildcroft Manor was understandable if it was once conceded that they were the victims of blackmail.

The big man was very thoughtful when he entered his bare office and sent for the file containing all that was known of the Marsh case. When it came he settled himself to study it; and by the time he had finished, and made certain notes, it was nearly one o'clock. He had lunch — his usual toast and tea — at the little tea-shop in Whitehall, and set off to make his first call.

George Devine's literary agent had an office in a turning off the Strand, and he greeted Mr. Budd with surprise which turned to horrified amazement when he learned that his profitable client had been murdered. It was the first intimation that he had had of such a thing, for it had been agreed between the superintendent and Tipman that the author's death should not be made public as yet.

'Dear, dear, this is terrible news,' exclaimed Mr. Winter. 'Terrible news! His new book comes out next month, too.' And then he brightened a little. 'It'll be a grand advertisement, though.'

'No doubt he thought of that when he allowed himself to be killed, sir,' said Mr. Budd. 'What I want to know is, what was his average income?'

The literary agent was reluctant to divulge this, but after Mr. Budd had patiently pointed out that it was necessary for the police to know, in view of certain investigations that were being made, he grudgingly gave the information that was required. The big man noted it down, obtained the name of Devine's bank, and took his leave.

At the bank he received some interesting details concerning Devine's account. It was not so large as it should have been, according to what he had learned from the literary agent. In fact it was extremely small.

'Mr. Devine was in the habit of drawing out very large amounts,' said the manager in explanation of this. 'Very large amounts indeed.'

'Who to?' asked Mr. Budd.

'His cheques were usually made out to self,' was the reply. 'Though what he did with so much money, I haven't the least idea — the amounts were never less than five thousand pounds, and often considerably more.'

Mr. Budd probed and questioned, and by five o'clock that afternoon had collected a vast amount of queer information about the people concerned in this extraordinary case. At six o'clock he went back for a further interview with Trainor. That individual was sitting morosely in the bare little cell, and scarcely even troubled to look up when he came in.

'Now, Mr. Trainor,' said the big man, 'I want to have another little talk with you, and I'm going to talk pretty straight. When I saw you this mornin' I asked you a question which you wouldn't answer. I'm going to ask you that question again, and you can please yourself whether you tell me what I want to know or not. What hold had Hebert Marsh over you?'

'I don't understand what you're talking about,' said Trainor. 'I told you that before.'

'I think you do, sir,' said Mr. Budd slowly. 'I think you understand very well indeed. If Marsh had no hold over you, why, for the last five years before his death, were you payin' him seven thousand pounds a year?'

Trainor looked up quickly, his face twitching. 'How did you find that out?' he asked.

'It came to light in the course of inquiries,' answered the detective evasively. 'So did other things, too, which are both interestin' and peculiar. Mr. Devine, for instance, was also in the habit of payin' large sums to Marsh.'

This was pure speculation on his part. He had no evidence where the money that Devine had drawn so regularly from his bank had gone. It was just a shot in the dark, but it hit the mark, as he could see by the expression on Trainor's face. 'Krayle was also one of Marsh's benefactors,' he continued. 'So, too, were Curtis and Hope. In fact every one of you, prior to Marsh's death, was in the habit of paying him large sums of money. Now I want to know why.'

With a weary gesture Trainor leaned back on the truckle bed. Fumbling in his pocket he produced a cigarette, and held out his hand. 'Give me a match,' he said.

Mr. Budd complied with the request, and the other lit his cigarette and blew out a cloud of smoke, smiling ruefully. 'We paid because we had to,' he said, replying to the detective's last question. 'We paid because Marsh had us like that.' He clenched his hand. 'You thought we were all friends of his, didn't you! So we were, outwardly, but it was he who sought us out.' He gave a hard little laugh.

'Friends! Victims would be a better word. I didn't want to tell you this, for Cathleen's sake — for all our sakes. I would rather have kept silent, but you seem to know so much that you've forced my hand.' He paused, drew hard at the cigarette, and inhaled the smoke. 'Listen,' he said, exhaling a long breath, 'Hebert Marsh was a blackmailer — a blackmailer of the worst type'

If he expected any expression of surprise, he was disappointed. Mr. Budd merely nodded his head slowly. 'I guessed that,' he grunted. 'It was the only explanation that would account for everyone wantin' to hide the crime and let it drop. You all wanted to hush it up for your own sakes, didn't you? You was afraid of what might come out.'

'Yes, we were all afraid of that,' Trainor admitted. 'Otherwise when Miss Marsh issued her invitation we should have refused. Under the circumstances, however, we dared not. We each suspected the other of having killed Marsh, and we were afraid not to turn up for fear of causing suspicion, and also in case anything should be discovered about us.'

'How do you mean?' asked the superintendent.

'Well,' said Trainor, 'Marsh held certain documents concerning the various indiscretions for which he'd got us under his thumb; and these, as you know, were never found. We didn't know where he kept them, but after his death we never knew when they might come to light. Of course, when you discovered that safe at the Witches' Moon, we knew where they were.'

'I see,' grunted Mr. Budd, stroking the lowest of his many chins. 'Tell me, Mr. Trainor, was the hold he had on you of a criminal nature?'

The young man shook his head. 'No,' he replied, 'it was a youthful piece of folly, but it would have created a terrible scandal had it become public property; a scandal that would have involved other people besides myself.' He hesitated. 'There was a woman mixed up in it, and she is married now.'

'I understand,' the big man broke in quickly. 'It is a pity you didn't take me into your confidence before, Mr. Trainor. The police are very lenient in blackmail cases. There was no reason why this indiscretion of yours shouldn't have been hushed up.'

'If I'd only had myself to think about, I should have told you,' said Trainor, 'but there were others to consider. For Miss Marsh's sake I didn't want to expose her father; and, naturally, I don't know what hold he had on the others. Some of them may have done something criminal which, if it had become known, would have forced the police to take action. You must agree that I was in rather an awkward position.'

'Yes, I suppose you was,' said Mr. Budd. 'Still, you'd 'uv saved a lot of trouble if you'd only been candid, and maybe three lives,' he added. 'How long had Marsh been blackmailing you?'

'For over five years,' replied Trainor. 'Once every three months he used to invite me down to Wildcroft Manor, and there I'd hand over two thousand five hundred pounds in notes. I didn't know that the others who were there were on the same errand until some time afterwards.'

'Was his sister there on these occasions?' asked Mr. Budd, and Trainor nodded.

'Always,' he replied. 'So were Krayle and Curtis. Devine and Hope didn't start coming until later.'

'And you've no idea who killed him?' asked the fat man.

Trainor looked uneasy.

'Now come along, sir,' urged Mr. Budd. 'If you've any idea it's your duty to speak.'

'I've no real proof,' muttered the other, 'only a suspicion.'

'About who?'

'I'm not going to say!' Trainor declared stubbornly. 'Even if I knew definitely, I wouldn't say. Marsh thoroughly deserved to die, and I wouldn't help to send the person who killed him to the gallows.'

And to this he stuck, and all the cajoling and persuasion on the part of Mr. Budd wouldn't shift him.

'I s'pose you know you can be accused of bein' an accessory if you hide up what you know!' he warned at last.

'I don't know anything!' was the quick retort. 'And I'm not bound to say what I think.'

This was true, and so Mr. Budd had no reply to make. Just as he was going, Trainor looked up. 'What about this charge?' he asked.

'You mean breaking into Marsh's house?' said the big man, and the other nodded.

'Yes, can't you squash it, or arrange something?' he said. 'It will only cause an unholy scandal if I'm brought up before the magistrate, and do no good to anybody.'

Mr. Budd considered for a moment. 'If I do,' he said after a pause, 'you must come back with me to the manor.'

Trainor shrugged his shoulders. 'I'm quite willing to do that,' he agreed. 'Only get me out of this wretched place.'

The superintendent went back to the charge-room and got through to Scotland Yard. After a short conversation he hung up the receiver and turned to the desk-sergeant. 'Mr. Trainor is to be released,' he said. 'I will take full responsibility.'

The grizzled sergeant nodded, and when Mr. Budd left Carlboro' Street Police Station, Gerald Trainor went with him.

'You can stay with me tonight,' said the big man. 'We'll go down to the manor first thing in the mornin'.'

Trainor accepted the invitation, and slept more comfortably in the spare bedroom at Mr. Budd's little house at Streatham than he had done on the previous night.

It was still dark when he was awakened by somebody shaking his shoulder, and looking sleepily up, he saw his host standing fully dressed by the bedside.

'Get up and dress yourself, sir,' said Mr. Budd harshly. 'We're goin' down to Wildcroft Manor at once.'

'You're going early,' grumbled Trainor, still only half awake.

'I am, and it's necessary,' snapped the superintendent. 'I've just had a telephone message relayed from the Yard. Mr. Rutherford rang up. Miss Marsh has disappeared.'

12

The Message

'Now, sir,' said Mr. Budd gravely, 'I'd like you to tell me all you know about this.'

He and Trainor had made a record journey from London, and had arrived at Wildcroft Manor just as dawn was breaking. They had been met by the lawyer, and now stood in the gloomy lounge waiting to hear what he had to say.

'I'm afraid there's very little to tell you,' began Rutherford with a worried frown. 'I went to bed early last night and fell asleep almost at once. About three I was awakened by some sound that I couldn't quite place. I think it was the howling of a cat. I had just turned over with the intention of going to sleep again when I heard another sound. It seemed to me like the soft closing of a door. I got up, and slipping into my clothes, came out of my bedroom and listened. Everything was

241

quite silent, and it was very cold. I crept to the head of the staircase, but there was nobody about at all, and yet I could have sworn I had heard a door shut softly. I was on the point of returning to my room when I felt a draught blowing from somewhere. Then I saw that the door to Miss Marsh's room was open.

'I was rather surprised at first, but I thought perhaps she had gone in to her aunt, and that *that* was the door I had heard close. The draught, however, was coming strongly from her room, and I went across and tapped on the partly opened door. There was no answer, and after a second I looked in. The room was in darkness, but the window was wide open. I could dimly see the bed, and it was unoccupied, although it had been slept in, for the clothes were tumbled about.

'I was beginning to feel alarmed, and I went and listened at Miss Emily Marsh's door, but there was no sound at all from within. I tried the handle and found that the door was locked. Miss Marsh could hardly be with her aunt, or I should have heard some sound; besides which, it was unlikely she would have locked the door. I went back to my room for a box of matches, and then I returned to Miss Marsh's room. There I found traces of muddy footprints on the floor by the window, and what was more startling — this!' He took from his pocket a folded piece of cloth. 'You can still smell it,' he said, holding it out to Mr. Budd, 'although it is much fainter than it was.'

The big man took the pad from his hand and put it to his nose. There was no mistaking the sickly-sweet odour. It was chloroform! 'Where in the room did you find this?' he asked.

'By the side of the bed,' replied Rutherford, 'the side nearest the window.'

Mr. Budd nodded, his heavy lids drooping over his eyes until they were almost completely closed. 'Go on, sir,' he prompted. 'What did you do next?'

'I alarmed the house,' said the lawyer, 'but nobody could throw any light on Miss Marsh's disappearance. Nobody had heard anything, or at least they said they hadn't. I searched about outside as well as I could in the dark, but I found nothing; and then I searched the whole house, with the same result. There was no sign of Miss Marsh anywhere. Then I went to the nearest call box and rang up Scotland Yard.'

'Did you get in touch with the local police?' asked the superintendent.

'Yes,' said Rutherford, 'and told Inspector Tipman what had happened. He's combing the district at the moment to try and find some trace of Miss Marsh.'

Mr. Budd pursed his lips. 'I'll have a look at the bedroom,' he said curtly, and went out into the hall.

'This is dreadful!' said Trainor agitatedly, following close on his heels. 'Who could have wanted to harm Cathleen?'

The big man made no reply. Breathing noisily, he hurried up the stairs, and at the open doorway of the woman's bedroom stopped and peered in.

There was no doubt that she had left hurriedly. The bedclothes were thrown back as though she had started up suddenly on being awakened, and the pillow was dented more so than it would have been by a normal sleeper. Looking,

Mr. Budd could picture what had happened almost as though he had seen it enacted. Somebody had come in stealthily by the window, and the woman had awakened and started up in alarm. But before she could cry out, the pad of chloroform had been pressed down over her mouth and nostrils and held there until she had lost consciousness . . .

The question was — who had been the assailant, and where had she been taken?

The superintendent entered the room and looked about him. The muddy prints that Rutherford had mentioned were plainly visible, although they only showed on the strip of polished flooring between the edge of the carpet and the window — smears of yellow clay that showed up distinctly on the dark wood.

He searched the room thoroughly, but there was no clue to the abductor. Except for the pad of cloth, he had left nothing behind him. Finishing his investigations at length, he turned to Rutherford and Trainor. 'There's nothing to be learned here,' he said. 'We'd better have a look round outside.'

The others assented, and he transferred his attention to the outside of the house, but with no better result. Near the fringe of the little wood was a strip of soft ground, and this was composed of the same clay soil that showed on the floor of the bedroom. Here he found several footprints, but they were of little or no value since they were only visible at that point, and therefore as a trail were useless.

He returned to the house, where he sent for everybody and closely questioned them. The latest development had filled them with a new fear, but it had not had the effect of loosening their tongues. They answered his questions sullenly and reluctantly, and the net result was exactly nothing.

'We must do something!' cried Gerald Trainor. 'This is terrible!'

'What do you suggest we should do, sir?' asked Mr. Budd, and the other made a gesture of despair.

'I don't know!' he said. 'But surely there's something.'

'The police are searchin' the district,' said the big man. 'Miss Marsh can't have been taken very far — she wasn't even dressed. Her clothes are still on the chair where she left them when she went to bed, so it looks as though she must be somewhere close at hand.'

'If she's still alive!' muttered Trainor, his face grey.

'I don't think you need worry about that, sir,' said Mr. Budd quietly. 'I think she's safe enough.'

'What do you mean?' Trainor looked his surprise.

'What I say,' replied the detective. 'No harm will come to Miss Marsh — yet!'

At that moment Pullman came into the lounge, his face yellower than usual, a square white object held in his hand. 'I've just found this!' he said, approaching Mr. Budd. 'It must've been pushed under the kitchen door, sir.' He held out the white thing, and they saw that it was an envelope, dirty and crumpled.

'It is addressed to you,' said the butler, 'though where it came from I haven't the least idea.'

Mr. Budd took it and frowned at the superscription. His name had been roughly printed in ink. With a thumb he ripped open the flap and drew out the single sheet of paper the envelope contained. His exclamation drew Gerald Trainor to his side, and they stared down at the message roughly scrawled in printed characters:

'CATHLEEN MARSH IS SAFE AT PRESENT. IT'S UP TO YOU WHETHER SHE REMAINS SO. LEAVE THE MARSH BUSINESS ALONE. KEEP OUT AND STAY OUT OR IT WILL BE THE WORSE FOR HER.'

There was no signature.

* * *

Cathleen Marsh remembered very little of the events of the night, when she recovered consciousness. She had awakened suddenly from a sound sleep to feel an icy wind blowing around her room, and to see, dimly, a shadowy figure creeping towards her bed.

Starting up in terror, which the sight inspired, she had opened her mouth to scream, but before the sound could leave her throat the stealthy shape had sprung forward. Something wet and cold and sickly-smelling had been forced over her mouth and nose and held there until her senses had drifted away.

When she recovered them again she was lying in total darkness; and when the first feeling of physical sickness had passed and she tried to move, she found that she had been securely bound. She had no idea where she was or how long she'd been there. The air around her was damp, and smelt earthy and stale. Her fingers touched the floor, and she felt the dank, cold surface of stone. Her intelligence told her that she was somewhere underground — but where?

She had seen nothing of the man or men who had brought her to this place, and was completely unable to imagine who it could be, or for what reason she had been kidnapped. With all her heart she wished now that she had left well alone and had not made her attempt to probe into the mystery surrounding her father's death.

Her plan, which had seemed so good when she had first conceived it, had brought nothing in its train but death and disaster. The use of the word 'train' switched her mind to Gerald Trainor. It was on his account chiefly that she had taken this foolhardy step, and tried to discover the real murderer of her father. She had to know which of those people who had been present was guilty, for Trainor had asked her to marry him, and unless she knew he was guiltless she could not give him the answer he wanted, or that she wished to give. It would be impossible to marry a man while the slightest suspicion still lingered that his hands were stained with blood.

The pain in her head had subsided to a dull ache but the nausea had completely gone. She would, at that moment, have given almost anything for a cup of tea, and began also to realise that she was getting hungry.

She was a very ordinary, sensible woman, without the slightest trace of the modern complaint of hysteria in her composition; and she began to wonder, quite calmly, what was going to happen. She was rather surprised herself at her calmness. She had no illusions regarding the people she had to deal with. They had killed already to preserve their secret — whatever it was — and certainly would not hesitate to kill again if it suited them.

A sound broke in on her thoughts, and moving her eyes to where it came from she saw a slit of light appear in the darkness. There was a squeaking sound, and the thread of light widened as a door was opened. She made out the vague figure of a man at the top of a flight of broken wooden stairs. He was carrying a lighted hurricane lamp, held high above his head, and coming slowly down the steps he set the lamp on the floor and advanced towards her.

He was wearing an overcoat and hat, and his face was hidden by a handkerchief that was bound loosely round nose and chin. He looked down at her for some minutes in silence; and then, from the pocket of his coat, he took a long-barrelled pistol and bent forward. She felt a momentary shiver of fear as she saw the weapon. Had he come to kill her? Her fears appeared groundless, for he only loosened the gag and pulled it away from her mouth.

'It's no good you shouting or screaming,' he muttered gruffly. 'No one will hear you. I have brought you some food.'

With his left hand he dragged out of his pocket a packet of sandwiches and a thermos-flask. Propping her up against the wall, he unscrewed the top and held the flask to her lips. It contained hot coffee, and she drank greedily.

'Now eat some of these.' He fed her with the sandwiches, holding them so as to avoid undoing the cords at her wrists. While she ate she took stock of her surroundings in the dim light of the lantern.

The place to which she had been brought was a fairly large cellar. The walls were of white-washed brick, and she could see the roof of thick, heavy, rough-hewn beams. There was a queer whitish dust over everything. On the floor it was inches thick, and there were many lines of footprints that ran towards the rickety stairway.

There was a heap of what at first she took to be sacking, but which proved, she eventually saw with a thrill of curiosity, to be a human being — a woman! The man saw the direction of her eyes and grunted.

'Don't you bother about her,' he said. 'Didn't know you'd got company, eh? Well, you 'ave!'

'Who is it?' she asked.

'It's no concern of yours,' he retorted. 'She's been here for some time now, and she's likely to be here longer.'

'Where is this place?' she asked. 'Why have I been brought here?'

'Not much of a place, is it?' he said. 'Don't you worry where it is — you're all right up to now, ain't yer? And you'll continue to be all right if certain people do as they're told.'

'Suppose they don't?' she said.

The man brushed some crumbs off his coat and shrugged his shoulders. 'Then you'll be all wrong!' he said; and before she could reply to this, he stooped and picked up the gag, refastened it, and, taking the lamp, went out. The door closed behind him with a bang, and she heard the rasp of a key followed by the thud of shooting bolts.

Who was her companion? She had caught the faintest glimpse of greying hair. An elderly woman — but who? She had been unable to see her face, but she had noted that she was gagged, too. Who could this woman be who was being kept a prisoner and who, according to her informer, had been there for some time?

She was still puzzling her brains when she fell asleep.

13

Found!

Gerald Trainor paced restlessly up and down the floor of his bedroom, too worried to think of sleep. The rest of that day, after he and Mr. Budd returned to Wildcroft Manor, had been a nightmare. Only by a great effort had he forced himself to act at all rationally. The disappearance of Cathleen and the certainty of her danger was a constant gnawing canker at the root of his mind. The shock at first had been so great that it had dulled his senses, but now its effect was wearing off, and full realisation was taking its place.

The utter helplessness of his own position did nothing to relieve the strain. If only he could evolve some form of action, it would have provided an anodyne, but he couldn't. His mind went on and on, working in circles, until his eyes were hot and heavy and there was a dull throbbing pain in his temples.

The rest of the people in that gloomy house became unbearable to him. Mr. Budd had gone out and had remained out. Rutherford, as worried as himself, offered nothing in the way of companionship. And so, at an early hour, Trainor had betaken himself to his own room to start that ceaseless, aimless pacing up and down, until it became merely an unconscious movement of the muscles. Subconsciously he heard the rest of the household retire for the night — voices whispered, footsteps passed his door — and then gradually the sounds ceased and silence settled down on the house.

The big clock in the hall struck twelve in measured, muffled strokes that drifted faintly to his ears, and after the lapse of what seemed ages — one, half-past one, two . . . up and down, up and down . . . a monotonous patrol from the door to the window and back again. He lost all sense of time, and realised with a start that dawn was breaking. He threw open the window and looked out, inhaling deep draughts of the sweet early-morning air.

Everything was very still, with that curious stillness and solemnity which is the attribute of early morning.

For a long time he let the coolness soothe his burning forehead; and then, withdrawing his head, he went over the wash-basin, splashed some water into the basin, and laved his face. As he was drying himself he heard the noise of a car. It came closer, and he guessed that the machine had turned into the drive. Going back to the window he leaned out, but the trees screened his view and he could see nothing. Then from below came the jangling of a bell, an impatient summons that after a second or two was repeated.

He heard a door open and close and hurried, shuffling footsteps. After that there was an interval of silence, and then the sound of voices. Something was happening! Had anything been found? He went quickly over to the door, jerked it open, and hurried into the dark corridor, almost colliding with somebody just outside. It was Mr. Budd! The big man was fully dressed. Evidently he, too, had found sleep impossible.

'What's happened?' demanded Trainor, clutching his arm.

'I don't know yet,' growled the superintendent. 'I'm just goin' to find out.'

He went ponderously down the stairs with Trainor at his heels. The front door was open and Pullman, scantily attired in a faded dressing gown over his pyjamas, was talking to a uniformed policeman who stood just within the open front door. He turned at Mr. Budd's approach.

'This man wants to see you, sir,' he said. 'I was just coming up to tell you.'

'What is it?' demanded the superintendent.

The constable saluted respectfully. 'Inspector Tipman sent me, sir; we've found the lady!'

'Found her? Where?' demanded Mr. Budd.

'At Marling's Mill, sir,' answered the policeman. 'It's an old place — been empty for years — about six miles from here. The inspector's waiting there for you. He said I was to bring you back with me.'

'Right, I'll come at once,' said Mr. Budd, and jerked his hat and coat off the hall-stand.

'Can I come with you?' put in Trainor quickly.

The big man hesitated. 'No, I don't think you'd better,' he said.

'But, damn it man — ' protested the other.

'Yes, I know all you're goin' to say!' broke in the superintendent. 'And I sympathize with your point of view, but just you be patient; I don't want too many people messin' around. Miss Marsh is safe, an' that ought to satisfy you to be goin' on with. Now then, let's go,' he added, and followed the constable to the waiting car.

Marling's Mill was a dilapidated old building standing on the crest of a hill. The gaunt sweeps had long since decayed, so that only a few wooden spars showed.

At the entrance Tipman was standing waiting for them, and he hailed Mr. Budd with an expression of relief. 'Glad you've come,' he grunted. 'We've found them both. Miss Marsh is well and unhurt, but the other is in rather a bad way.'

The big man looked at him with raised brows. 'Other? What other?' he demanded.

'There was another woman there,' said

Tipman. 'An elderly, grey-haired woman. I don't know who she is. You'd better come and see them.' He led the way into the grinding chamber, a place of rusty machinery and broken stone rollers.

Cathleen Marsh, dusty and dishevelled, was sitting on a rotting packing case, with the inspector's overcoat draped over her shoulders. She smiled as she saw Mr. Budd.

'Did you recognise the man who brought you here?' he asked, when she had briefly told her story.

She shook her head. 'No!' she replied; and then, after a momentary hesitation: 'But his face seemed familiar somehow, although I can't say who he reminded me of.'

'That's a pity,' remarked the big man, and turning to Tipman: 'Where's this other woman you were talkin' about?'

The inspector pointed to a door which had once, apparently, led to a kind of office. 'In there,' he answered. 'She's unconscious, so you won't get anything out of her yet.'

'I don't want to!' said Mr. Budd. 'I only want to see her.' He went across to the smaller room and bent over the pile of sacks that lay on the floor. Amid them was a middle-aged, grey-haired woman. Her thin face was pale and drawn, and she was breathing heavily.

'Drugged!' commented the big man, and his eyes were narrowed to slits. 'Well, I think this solves our mystery!'

'Why? Who is she? Do you know?' demanded Tipman.

'I don't know, but I can guess now I've seen her,' answered Mr. Budd; and then: 'Ask Miss Marsh to come here, will you?'

The woman came, clasping the inspector's coat round her.

'D'you know this lady, Miss Marsh?' said the superintendent, when she stood by his side.

She down, and looking, caught her breath. 'Oh, it's impossible — impossible!' she breathed incredulously. 'It can't be — ' She whispered a name, and Mr. Budd nodded.

'It is!' he said. 'There's no doubt in my mind.' He looked across at the amazed Tipman. 'Tell the constable to stay here and look after her,' he said, pointing to the unconscious figure on the rug. 'We'll be gettin' back to Wildcroft Manor and play out the last act in this drama in the same settin' in which it began.'

* * *

It was a dull day, and the leaping flames of the log fire filled the lounge at Wildcroft Manor with an uncertain light — a light that caused grotesque dancing shadows of ever-changing shapes on the walls and ceiling, and lit up the faces of the people present with a shifting glare. The faces were tense and expectant, with more than a trace of fear in some of them, and the eyes of all were watchful and wary as they stared at Mr. Budd.

The big man had brought Cathleen Marsh and the elderly woman back to the manor, and succeeded in smuggling them in so that no one was the wiser. When he had done this he had sent Tipman to everybody with a request that they should all gather in the lounge — and here they were, a scared, silent community, wondering a little fearfully what it was all about.

Mr. Budd left them very little time to speculate, for as soon as they were grouped round the fire he addressed them, taking up a position in the centre of the room beside Inspector Tipman.

'A few days ago,' he began, 'I was invited by Miss Cathleen Marsh to stay here for the weekend. She had some idea in her mind that by gettin' everybody down who had been present when her father was killed, somethin' might come to light that would clear up the mystery surroundin' his death. I don't know what her object was, but I accepted the invitation after consultation with my chief, and on the night of my arrival another murder was committed. Mr. Krayle was shot dead in the same room in which Hebert Marsh had been killed three years before.' He paused, letting his sleepy eyes rove from one white, drawn face to another, but nobody spoke.

Pullman, standing beside Mary Hutton, shuffled his feet slightly. Emily Marsh uttered a sound that was like a stifled cough, but that was all; the rest remained rigid, intent, expectant.

'There was no clue to the murderer,' the superintendent went on, 'except that it was fairly obvious it was someone in the house.'

This time there was a little gasp — a quick indrawing of breath — and it came from Alice Devine, but Mr. Budd took no notice, and continued rapidly: 'There were several curious incidents attachin' to this second crime. A book containin' a scrawled verse on the flyleaf was stolen from the room in which Krayle lay dead, an' it wasn't only stolen once, it was stolen twice! The first time, I think, by Mr. Devine, and the second time from under my pillow where I had put it after findin' it in the coal-scuttle, by the murderer.'

He looked across at Emily Marsh, from whose tight lips a faint sound had come, but went on almost immediately. 'When the murderer failed to find in it what he wanted — the flyleaf which had been taken out by Mr. Devine — he put it back in the dead man's room; but somebody had taken away an old fireman's helmet. It looked as if an exchange had been made, but I don't think anythin' of the sort happened, because the helmet was found later up the chimney in Mr. Devine's room, and I think he'd taken it earlier because the inscription on it and the verse in the book formed a clue to the whereabouts of a safe belongin' to Hebert Marsh.

'Krayle died because he was in possession of that book. He'd taken it at the time of the Marsh murder, and he knew that the verse scrawled on the flyleaf showed where Marsh had put his safe, but he didn't know the connection between the verse and the helmet. Devine died by the same hand because he had discovered the connection, and knew of that safe which was hidden in the Witches' Moon. All this was the outcome of the first murder, the killin' of Hebert Marsh. Marsh was killed for a reason that you all know and have been constantly tryin' to hide.'

There was a little stirring among his audience, like the sudden rising of a wind dispersing dead leaves.

'Hebert Marsh was a blackmailer!' he

said slowly. 'He blackmailed every one of you, an' his wealth was the outcome of money he had wrung from each of you when he invited you down here for those periodical weekends. In that safe, which you were all so reluctant should be opened, he kept the evidence which he used to squeeze this revenue from you. I don't think, with the exception of his sister, that any of you knew of its existence, or knew where he kept the documents that enabled him to live at ease on your money.'

'We didn't — God knows we didn't!' The interruption came from Alice Devine. Her face was chalk-white, and she was staring at him with white, hot eyes. 'If we had — ' She broke off and Mr. Budd nodded slowly.

'If you had,' he said, 'some of you would have tried to get 'em. That is why Marsh chose such an unlikely place to hide the safe, an' also arranged it so that it couldn't be opened without risk of an explosion, except by usin' the proper combination. However, we'll leave that for the moment. We've got as far as the motive for killin' Marsh and the motive for killin' Krayle and Devine. What we're comin' to now is not why these crimes were committed, but who committed 'em.' He looked keenly from face to face.

Emily Marsh was staring at the floor, her face expressionless. Alice Devine kept her large eyes fixed on him, and twisted and untwisted a wisp of handkerchief in her lap. Pullman, his face a dirty grey, was licking his dry lips and darting sharp little glances from one to the other. The stolid Mary Hutton remained impassive. Trainor was biting his nails impatiently and shifting nervously in his chair. Lionel Hope sat quietly staring at the fire, the big lenses of his glasses obliterating all trace of expression. Leslie Curtis sprawled on the settee, a cigarette that had gone out drooping from his thin lips, and a rather overdone bored expression on his good-looking face.

There was an electrical tension in the atmosphere that was like the lull before the thunderclap that heralds the bursting of the storm.

'Yes,' repeated the big man slowly. 'That's what we're comin' to — the person who committed these crimes. The person who shot Hebert Marsh, an' shot Krayle; the person who stabbed Devine an' who also kidnapped and afterwards killed James Augustus Dench; the person who came down to Wildcroft Manor a day before Miss Marsh, an' the guests she had invited, an' took the place of an innocent woman . . . '

A smothered cry interrupted him; a sharp, stifled gasp. There was a sudden movement, a quick rush and: 'Stop him!' cried Mr. Budd sharply.

Tipman sprang forward and gripped the arms of the fleeing figure. Panting and wrenching at her arm to try and loosen the inspector's hold, Mary Hutton glared defiance at her captor, and a string of invectives flowed from her snarling lips.

'That'll do!' snapped Mr. Budd sternly, and stepping forward he jerked off the grey wig, revealing the dark, close-cropped head of a man.

14

An Accusation!

The other people gathered in the room had started to their feet and were gaping in astonishment at the man between Tipman and Mr. Budd.

'Clever, ain't you?' he snarled, glaring at the big man. 'Bloody clever! But you've got the wrong man! I ain't no murderer!'

'We'll see what a jury has to say about that!' retorted Mr. Budd, and swung round as Emily Marsh tottered forward, her thin lips working, her hollow eyes wide and fearful. 'Harry,' she stammered. 'Harry, you — you — ' She stopped, and the dark man laughed harshly.

'Didn't expect to see me, did you, Emily?' he sneered. 'Didn't dream your husband was so near, eh? I'll bet you didn't!'

'Husband!' echoed the bewildered Mr. Budd.

The man called Harry twisted towards him swiftly. 'Yes, husband!' he snapped. 'You didn't know that, did you, Mr. Clever Dick? Well, you've learnt something. I married her ten years ago. She was better-looking then, but she was snobbish. She insisted on it being kept secret. Wouldn't have done for her swell friends to know that she'd married her brother's chauffeur, Harry Hutton . . . '

'Harry,' muttered the old woman. 'Harry!'

'Oh, go and sit down!' growled Hutton, and then, looking at Mr. Budd defiantly: 'Well, what are you going to do with me?'

'I'm goin' to arrest you,' said the superintendent grimly.

'What for?' demanded the other. 'Impersonating me own sister? She won't charge me, an' you've got nothing else against me.'

'I've got a charge of murder against you!' said Mr. Budd, 'an' I don't think you'll find it easy to wriggle out of. That's the main charge. There are others — forcible abduction, an' — '

'I didn't do the murders,' broke in

Hutton, 'and I only did the other things because I was forced to. I couldn't help meself. This wasn't my idea. I was made to do what I did — '

'Who by?' asked the big man sharply.

'By him!' cried the other, and the words had barely left his lips when a hard, metallic voice interrupted.

'Keep still, all of you!' it said crisply. 'Don't move! The first person who moves an eyelid is going to take a quick trip to hell!'

Mr. Budd swung round. Crouching by the door, his face white and set, a long-barrelled automatic gripped in his hand, was Leslie Curtis! In the general excitement he had left his place on the settee and, unnoticed, had made his way stealthily to the door.

'Don't move!' he repeated, 'or I'll fill you full of lead!' His left hand was fumbling with the door behind him as he spoke. 'Keep hold of Hutton,' he went on, 'because he's the only one you'll get, and there's enough evidence in that safe to send him down for a seven-years stretch — if you can get at it!'

He had found the key and taken it from the lock, and now he jerked open the door and backed into the hall. 'I'm taking your car,' he said, 'and I warn you not to try and follow me.'

The next second he was gone, the door slammed shut behind him, and they heard the key turn in the lock. Tipman turned swiftly to the window, but Mr. Budd caught his arm. 'Don't be a fool,' he growled. 'He's armed and we're not. We couldn't stop him.'

'But we can't let him get away!' protested the inspector.

As he spoke there came the sudden roar of a suddenly accelerated motor-engine, followed by the swish of tyres on gravel.

'He's *got* away,' grunted the big man as the noise of the engine diminished, 'for the moment. He won't get far, though. I wish this house was on the telephone.'

He pushed open the casement window and climbed out. The inspector's car still stood in the drive, but his own was gone. A hasty examination showed that Curtis had taken the precaution of slashing two of the tyres before driving away.

'You were a chauffeur once, weren't you?' he said, turning to the sullen-faced Hutton, whom Tipman had brought with him when he followed the big man through the window. 'Well, you can make yerself useful an' mend them tyres.'

'I'll see you in — ' began the man loudly, but Mr. Budd cut him short.

'You'll do as you're told!' he snapped. 'Now go on, get down to it!'

* * *

Leslie Curtis sped along the narrow, twisting road in Mr. Budd's ancient car as fast as that decrepit machine would allow. When he had seen that Hutton's disguise had been penetrated, he had realised that the man would give him away, and had been prepared. He had made his desperate bid for freedom, and it had come off.

What he had to do now was retain his liberty, and that was more difficult. It would only be a question of minutes before his description was broadcast all

273

over the country, and every policeman would be looking for him. It was useless, therefore, making for any railway station. He might succeed in boarding a train before the news went out, but wherever he left it, a vigilant watcher would be waiting.

It was equally useless to try and get away by road. The car would also be described, and was likely, in a short time, to be more of a liability than an asset. The best chance he had of making a getaway was to lie low somewhere until it was dark. But the difficulty was, where?

And then an idea came to him. Devil's Wood — that great tract of forestland that covered more than two hundred and fifty acres, and was shunned by the superstitious inhabitants of the surrounding district. He could get rid of the car and lie concealed in the wood until nightfall, and under cover of darkness there might be an opportunity for escape. Anyway, it was the best thing he could think of in the short time at his disposal. Somewhere he *must* hide, that was certain, and the wood offered the best hiding place. Every passing minute was fraught with danger while he remained in the open.

He turned the car into a side lane, ran halfway along it, and pulled up. Devil's Wood lay a mile to the south, and he remembered that there was a footpath skirting the fringe of a strip of common land that would bring him to it.

Abandoning the car, he set off as fast as he could walk, keeping a sharp lookout for any sign that would warn him of danger. But he saw nothing, and blessed the fact that there was no telephone at Wildcroft Manor. He reached the wood, breathless, and plunged into the shelter of the thickly growing trees.

Here was temporary safety. The police would never be able to search that vast belt of forest. He found a bracken-filled hollow and stopped to rest. When he had recovered his breath he considered his position. He had a chance. For the time being he had succeeded in getting away and, with a modicum of luck, he might turn that temporary advantage into a permanent one.

He saw a tall tree nearby, and climbing

it, took stock of his surroundings. A short distance away a narrow road wound towards Mallington, and where the wood began to thin he could see the broken chimneys of the Witches' Moon. The sight filled him with a sudden rage, and he only calmed himself with an effort. It was useless giving way to futile anger. His plans had gone wrong, and he was lucky to be free. For that he was thankful.

He wedged himself comfortably in a forked branch and watched the road. For a long time it remained deserted, and then he saw a car come speeding along from the direction of Mallington. It stopped a quarter of a mile away and three men got out. He could see the blue of their uniforms. So the hunt was up already? That fat, sleepy-eyed man whom he had regarded with contempt had succeeded in getting in touch with the police station at Mallington, had he? That meant that they would be looking for him; scouring the countryside and watching every road and railway station. He had been sensible to realise this danger, and take refuge in the wood. If he had tried to get out of the district at once he would have been caught for a certainty.

But there was still the problem of how he was going to get away from the wood, and it wasn't easily solved. The net would be spread wide, and it would be difficult to avoid. But not impossible. He had brains, and surely he could beat a lot of dunder-headed policemen?

But the day passed slowly, and night came down without his having evolved any feasible plan that would extricate him from his position. Leslie Curtis had no false ideas about the danger he was in. Although he had succeeded in outwitting Mr. Budd, he knew that he couldn't hope to remain free indefinitely unless he could think of some scheme that would enable him to get past the cordon that would be thrown around that stretch of country.

So long as he stayed out there in the wood itself, he was comparatively safe. There were countless places for a man to hide. But he couldn't stay there indefinitely. Hunger and thirst would, before very long, drive him into the arms of the very people he was so anxious to avoid.

Propping himself up against a fallen tree, he glanced at the luminous dial of his watch. He had nearly eight hours in which to think of something. In eight hours it would be getting light, and with the light his danger would be trebled. If only a fog would come up — such a fog as had enveloped the district on the night Marsh had died.

But the sky was clear and starry. There was no sign of anything of the sort. Perhaps, on second thought, it was just as well, for the fog would not only blind the men who were searching for him, but make it impossible for him to move.

He had very little money — scarcely four pounds all told, and that was not going to take him very far. There was no getting away from it — the case was a desperate one. There was money at his flat in London, but even should he succeed in getting away from this confounded wood, he would be mad to risk calling at his flat. That was the first place that would be put under observation.

And yet he would have to have money

from somewhere if he was to stand any chance of getting away. He searched his pockets for a cigarette, found a packet, and risked the momentary gleam of his lighter. The hollow would screen the light from being seen, and he had to smoke. He inhaled deeply, and the tobacco soothed his frayed nerves and set his brain working.

How the deuce could he take advantage of his luck in having dodged Budd, and get away? He smoked thoughtfully, his brows drawn together in a frown of concentration. When he had finished his cigarette he lit another from the stub, but rack his brains as he would, he could find no solution to his urgent problem.

It was an impossible situation. If only he could think of some means of disguise. Once he was away, safely out of the net which he knew was at that moment being spread in all directions to catch him, the money part of the problem might be solved. But every road from the district, every town and village, every railway station, would have vigilant watchers on the lookout for him, and he would be easily recognizable.

He came to the end of his stock of cigarettes and flung the empty packet away with a savage gesture. He might just as well face it. He was caught like a rat in a trap. There was *no* way. That confounded detective had known there was no way, and that was why he had abandoned the search so easily. The cold night air began to penetrate his thin clothes — he had neither overcoat nor hat; there had been no time for them in that mad dash for freedom and safety — and presently he found himself shivering violently. Damn that fat brute!

He had imagined that he was quite safe, and now all his elaborate scheming, all his carefully thought-out plans had tumbled to ruins about his head. He was an outcast — a hunted thing — the same as any little sneak-thief who had pinched a handbag. Except — and the thought sent a more violent shiver through him than the cold — except that if he was caught he would hang!

There was no doubt about that — nothing could save him from suffering the extreme penalty of the law, not even the cleverest counsel in the world. The evidence of Hutton would be fatal.

The cold was getting worse. A faint, biting wind was blowing across the open country — the wind that heralded the dawn. Already the sky in the east had lost its indigo and was slowly lightening. Slowly, and almost imperceptibly, but very surely.

He shifted into a warmer position, and as he moved he felt the hard shape of the automatic in his hip pocket pressing into his flesh. Well, anyhow, *there* was one way out. Better a flash of flame, an instantaneous searing of hot lead, than the long drawn-out agony of the trial, with its foregone conclusion.

He drew the little weapon from his pocket and pulled back the jacket. It was fully loaded. He remembered putting in the fresh clip of cartridges that morning. Was it only that morning? It seemed centuries ago. It was a comfortable feeling to have it, although he wouldn't use it until every hope had gone.

Every hope! There wasn't very much

hope, anyway, but still you never could tell. A miracle might happen. Who was it who had said that the most wonderful thing about miracles was that they sometimes happened?

He pulled himself up sharply. This would never do. He was wasting what few hours were left, trying to remember quotations when he ought to be racking his brains to find a way out. He wasn't a fool. After all, surely he was as clever as the police. Of course there was a way out, if he could only think of it. There was always a way out of everything . . .

He wished he had a cigarette left. Funny how one always wanted a thing more if it was unattainable.

The blueness in the east was turning grey — a long streak, like a horizontal sword. If only he could concentrate instead of letting his mind flit from one thing to another. He was tired — that was what it was. He was so tired that his weary brain refused to obey him. It would never do to let that tiredness get the better of him. If ever he had wanted to be wide awake, it was now. He must think

— think — think —

He woke with a start, and his forehead, in spite of the coldness of the early morning, became dewed with sweat. In the midst of his determination not to, he had fallen asleep, and he must have slept for some time, for the grey sword had changed to a flaming spear of crimson — or a streak of blood smudged across the horizon by a giant finger.

Stiffly, for his limbs were frozen and numb, he got to his feet. From the cover of the trees he could see along the road, and coming towards him was a fast-moving speck — a man on a bicycle. He watched the fast-moving little blot with haggard eyes, and presently saw that it was a policeman. So the cyclist patrols were out, covering the roads.

He crouched back into the shelter of the bushes, taking up a position so that he could still see the approaching cyclist — and then, suddenly, it flashed to his mind that here was the answer to the question that had puzzled his brains throughout the day and night; the miracle that sometimes happened.

He looked swiftly up and down the ribbon of road. There was no other living thing in sight, and his eyes glittered and his lips compressed into a hard, thin line. He took the automatic from his hip pocket, thumbed back the safety catch, and then, leaving his place of concealment, walked swiftly towards the road. By the time he reached it he calculated that the policeman would have drawn level with him.

The man, quite a young constable, saw him when he was still a hundred yards away, and shouted to him to stop. Leslie Curtis smiled grimly and waited. The policeman braked his machine, and dismounting came towards him. There was a triumphant grin on his red face.

'Got yer, 'ave I?' he cried exultantly. 'Well, this be a bit of luck fer me — '

'Don't be too sure of that, my friend,' snarled Curtis, and the hand holding the pistol came out from behind his back. 'Keep still and do as I tell you, or I'll drill you full of holes.'

The triumphant smile died from the policeman's face, and he looked foolishly at the menacing muzzle of the little pistol.

'Take off your helmet,' ordered Curtis, coming a step or two nearer.

The constable hesitated. He was unused to this sort of thing. Up to now he had only had to deal with tramps, and chicken stealers, and small boys, into whose souls the mere sight of him had brought terror. This was beyond his experience — this grim-faced man with the desperate eyes, and hard mouth, and the little black circle of death that showed over the fingers of his hand.

'Quick!' repeated Leslie Curtis harshly, and his right forefinger tightened on the trigger. The constable saw the movement and hesitated no longer. His hand went up and bared his reddish-brown head.

'That's right,' said Curtis, approaching until he was within two feet of his captive.

'Look 'ere,' began the policeman, and that was all he had time to say, for with a lightning movement Curtis shifted the pistol so that he gripped it by the barrel and brought the butt down with all the force of his muscular arm on the policeman's unprotected head. The man gave a little gasp and dropped.

Leslie Curtis pocketed the pistol and gave a sharp look round. The road was still deserted, and stopping, he picked up the unconscious form of the policeman and carried it over to the wood. Dumping it down, he went back and retrieved the bicycle, trundling it back to the cover of the trees, and then he began to work swiftly and feverishly. In less than two minutes he had stripped the policeman of his uniform and boots.

The man's shirt he took off and tore into strips, and with these he bound him securely, ending by stuffing a lump of grass into his mouth and binding it in place so that it formed an effective gag. When he had done this he began to remove his own clothing and dress himself in the constable's uniform. It was a fairly good fit, for the two men were almost the same build — the boots were a little large, but that was a detail.

When he had finished and adjusted the helmet, Leslie Curtis had disappeared, and in his place was a young policeman. The helmet concealed, to a great extent, the difference of features.

He rolled his own clothes into a bundle and stuffed them under a patch of bracken, dragged the bound and helpless body of his victim further into concealment, and after taking a last look round, picked up the bicycle and wheeled it towards the road.

The first pale yellow streaks of the rising sun were tingeing the sky with golden light as he mounted and pedalled off. With a bit of luck he might after all make good his escape, for unless he ran into someone who knew the man he was impersonating, his disguise was unlikely to be challenged.

He was feeling almost cheerful as he rode along, but there was one detail he had forgotten. It was a small mistake, but it was eventually to bring him to the gallows!

15

The Mistake

Mr. Budd sat before the blazing fire in the charge-room at Mallington police station, a black cigar gripped between his teeth, his brows corrugated in thought.

Throughout the night the wires had been humming with instructions to the outlying stations, and every road had its guard; every railway station was watchful for the appearance of the escaped murderer. The same system as that which is put into action when a convict escapes from the great prison at Princetown had been adopted, and the stout man knew that it was only a question of time before Leslie Curtis was caught in the net.

Hutton, no longer the truculent bully but a scared and thoroughly frightened man, was safely under lock and key. It was only the man who had been responsible — the man who had planned and directed the whole sinister business — who was still at large. Mr. Budd didn't envy him his thoughts and feelings. He must realise that escape was practically impossible, and that sooner or later starvation must force him into the open. Inspector Tipman came in from his private office, a greatly harassed and worried man.

'There's no news yet,' he said, warming his hands at the fire. 'But I don't see how he can slip through our fingers. I've got every available man on the job, and all the reserves have been called out.'

The big man threw away the stub of his cigar. 'I don't think you need worry, Tipman,' he remarked. 'I'm sure it's not possible for him to get away. It's only a question of waitin' patiently.'

The inspector nodded. 'I haven't left anything to chance,' he said. 'Unless he can make himself invisible, he hasn't a chance in hell of leaving the district.'

'Apart from his appearance,' said Mr. Budd, 'which, hatless an' coatless as he is, would be conspicuous anywhere. I don't s'pose he has much money, an' that will prove his greatest handicap.'

'Well, he won't be able to get any, even if he succeeded in doing the impossible and getting away from here,' grunted Tipman. 'I've already been in touch with London, and the police there have taken charge of his flat. His bank also has been notified. I think his guns are pretty well spiked.'

He went back to his office as the telephone rang, and through the open door Mr. Budd heard him issuing a further string of instructions to someone at the other end of the wire.

Well, he thought wearily, the case was nearly over, and he wasn't sorry. It had been a tedious business. It would be a long time before he would forget the atmosphere of that weird house and its weirder inmates — that grim and ghastly old woman, the fleshy-faced Alice Devine, and the rest of the strange bunch.

Cathleen Marsh, who would, of course, marry Gerald Trainor, would be well out of it. It was doubtful if she would ever set foot inside Wildcroft Manor again after this. The best thing she could do would be to sell the property — if she could find anyone to buy it — or, failing that, shut it up for good, and leave it to fall into decay. Yes, an ill-omened place, full of unpleasant memories and the residue of evil emotions.

And that safe? What would that reveal when it was opened? What soul-searing secrets did it contain? The hidden part of those people's lives that had brought them together under such strange circumstances, and kept them together because of their mutual fear.

In all his experience he couldn't recall a similar case. He had dealt with blackmail in nearly all its aspects — blackmail which to his mind was almost a worse crime than murder — but never in such a macabre setting or under such extraordinary circumstances.

Tipman finished his telephoning and came back again to the charge-room fire. 'Nothing yet,' he said, and Mr. Budd looked up with a yawn.

'You didn't expect there would be, did you?' he asked. 'You don't imagine that Curtis is goin' to make a bolt from wherever he's hidin' until he's compelled to for want of food?'

'That may mean waiting a couple of days,' the inspector grunted.

That's quite possible,' the big man agreed, 'unless one of your search parties stumble on him by chance. You never know. They may be lucky.'

At that moment the telephone rang again. The inspector disappeared once more into his office. The conversation was a short one, and then he burst into the charge-room excitedly. 'Come on!' he cried. 'They've got him!'

'Where did they get him?' asked the big man as he followed the other down the steps to the waiting car.

'On the London road,' said Tipman. 'There's a barricade there. He nearly got through, though. It was only one little mistake that stopped him.'

What was that?' asked Mr. Budd, and Tipman told him.

* * *

Leslie Curtis pedalled slowly along in the cold light of the morning, thinking out his plans as he went. So far so good. If by any chance he should meet anyone, they would take little notice of a solitary policeman; certainly, never for one moment would they dream that he was other than he appeared to be. And if he came across the cordon, he could say that he was on his way to the station to report.

With even a modicum of luck he ought to get away with it. The next question was money. How could he lay his hands on a sum that would be sufficient to get him out of the country? The keen air of the morning, acting as a tonic, stimulated his brain, and the plan came to him. Trainor, of course! Although the police would undoubtedly be watching his Curtis' flat, they wouldn't be watching Trainor's, and Trainor had once boasted that he always kept a supply of ready money in his desk in case of an emergency. As soon as he got clear he would make for London, go to Trainor's flat, and get hold of that money. Then he could lie low for a bit — until, say, he had grown a moustache and beard, or dyed his hair, before he attempted to leave the country.

Yes, there was a good chance. He felt much more optimistic now, and he had to thank that fool of a constable for putting in so opportune an appearance.

The sun had risen, and was bathing the countryside in primroses. The rays, feeble as yet, slanted across his path, and seemed to mutely utter a benediction. He'd do it! He'd outwit them all, yet!

He increased his speed slightly and, rounding a bend in the road, saw before him a car and a group of men. The barricade! Now was the time. A little bluff, and he was through. As he drew near, a sergeant stepped forward and held up his hand. Curtis halted, still remaining in his saddle, and saluted.

'I'm in a hurry, sir,' he said, his heart beating painfully. 'I've got a message to deliver to Inspector Tipman.'

'All right,' said the sergeant. 'What's the news? Have they found the fellow?'

'I couldn't tell you, sir,' said Curtis respectfully. 'I was asked by one of the sergeants in charge of a search party to tell Inspector Tipman to come back with me at once.'

'Sounds as if they'd found something,' commented the sergeant. 'All right, my lad, off you go.'

It had worked! His bluff had remained uncalled!

He saluted, and was just getting the cycle under way, when: 'Here, just a moment!' It was a young constable who spoke, and as he spoke he came running forward.

'What is it?' snapped the sergeant.

'There's something wrong here, sir,' said the constable. 'Look at that fellow's armlet.'

'What — ' began the sergeant, and then: 'By gosh! He's wearing it on the wrong arm!'

Curtis' heart gave a leap, and he glanced down at the circle of blue and white. He remembered it had fallen off. Had he put it on the wrong arm? He must have done — curse the thing!

'I'm sorry, sir,' he said aloud. 'I dressed very hurriedly.' He stopped.

The eyes that were surveying him were suspicious and hostile. A policeman's armlet, worn to signify that he is on duty,

295

would become so much a question of habit that it was impossible to believe that it could have been put on the wrong arm by accident.

'H'm! I'm not satisfied about you, my lad,' said the sergeant. 'You'll stay here until we've made some further inquiries. Jackson can take your message to the inspector.'

He laid his hand on Curtis' arm and the man lost his head. With a snarling oath, he leapt from the bicycle and flung it full at the sergeant. The latter staggered at the impact with the machine, and before he could recover his balance Curtis had taken to his heels.

He got nearly a fifty-yard start before the others came tearing in pursuit, but his sleepless night and the exposure to the cold had stiffened his limbs and cramped his muscles. A glance over his shoulder showed him that his pursuers were quickly gaining on him and, with a muttered oath, he snatched the pistol from his pocket and fired wildly at the lumbering, blue-clad forms.

The bullets went wide — his hand was

shaking so that it would have been surprising if they had done anything else. Again he fired, emptying the magazine in a sudden blind panic that swept over him like a surging sea. This was the end. He knew that he could never get away now; and yet, still with the instinct of self-preservation — the strongest of all human urges — he redoubled his efforts. His breath was coming in great panting gasps, whistling through his throat with a dry rattle.

A crimson curtain flecked with splashes of orange obscured his vision, and into his side came a stabbing pain like the thrust of a red-hot blade. With a curse he flung the empty pistol — which he suddenly discovered he was still holding — away from him, and then his foot caught in a rift in the ground and he fell headlong, badly wrenching his ankle.

Five seconds after that it was all over so far as he was concerned. His exertions and the pain made him lose consciousness, and when he recovered he found himself seated in a car beside Mr. Budd on the way to the police station. He only spoke once — just as they were approaching the outskirts of the town — and then, looking round at the detective, he said in a voice husky with pain and rage: 'I wish I hadn't mistaken you for a fool!'

Mr. Budd smiled sleepily. 'Quite a lot of people wish that,' he remarked.

*   *   *

Leslie Curtis was formally charged and consigned to a cell in Mallington police station, and it was a coincidence that he occupied the adjoining one to that of his accomplice, Hutton. The following day he would be taken to London to await his trial.

After the arrest Mr. Budd went back to the manor to say goodbye to Cathleen Marsh. His job was done, and he was anxious to return to London as soon as possible. He found the woman in the lounge talking to Sergeant Leek, who had returned during his absence, and she greeted him with the first genuine smile he had ever seen on her face.

'I'm so glad it's all over,' she said. 'You don't know what a terrible strain it's been, not knowing — who — '

'I can guess, miss,' interrupted the big man. 'I'm not sorry, myself. If I might say so, I should get away from this place as soon as you can.'

'I'm going back to London this afternoon,' she answered.

'That's fine!' said Mr. Budd. 'What's happened to the rest of 'em?'

'Mr. Hope has already gone,' she said. 'Mr. Trainor and Mr. Rutherford are coming up with Aunt Emily and me. Alice — Mrs. Devine — is packing.'

Almost as she spoke the door opened and the latter came in. 'How am I going to get my things to the station?' she demanded, taking no notice of Mr. Budd and the disconsolate Leek. 'I'm not expected to walk, am I?'

The superintendent was startled at the change in her. Her face had regained its firmness, and her eyes had lost the look of haunting fear that had lurked in their depths since he had first met her. The shrill edge had gone from her voice, leaving it hard and sullen; and, as if by magic, the lines about her mouth had been smoothed away. She was lavishly made up, and clearly the tragic death of her husband worried her not at all. All that concerned her was herself. No thought of anyone else troubled her mind. She was completely wrapped up in the welfare of Alice Devine.

'You brought me here,' she went on before Cathleen could reply, 'and it's up to you to see that I get away without inconvenience. I haven't got my car or — '

'I will see that there is a car to take you to the station,' replied Miss Marsh stiffly. 'When do you wish to go?'

'As soon as possible,' said the woman, and turning to Mr. Budd: 'There's no reason why I should be detained in this beastly place any longer, is there?'

'None, ma'am,' he answered shortly.

'Then I'd like to go at once,' she snapped.

'I'll send Pullman to hire a car — ' began Cathleen.

'There's no need to do that; I will drive

Mrs. Devine to the junction,' Rutherford's voice broke in quietly. He had come into the lounge without being heard.

Alice Devine did not even trouble to thank him. 'Then I'll get my things ready,' she said, and marched out of the room.

'Nice lady!' remarked the lawyer, shrugging his shoulders. 'Well, Superintendent, the case is over.'

'Except for knottin' up the threads,' Mr. Budd answered slowly. 'There's one or two loose ones that want properly tyin'.'

'Well, I'm damned glad,' said Rutherford. 'I don't want to spend another weekend like the last one in a hurry!'

'I don't think any of us do,' remarked Miss Marsh; and then abruptly: 'Would you like anything before you go?'

'Not for me, miss, thank you,' said the big man, shaking his head; but she insisted on ordering coffee.

Pullman did not appear in answer to the bell, and she went in search of him. When she came back she was accompanied by Emily Marsh. The gaunt woman looked even more forbidding than ever.

Her cheeks had fallen in, and the only things alive about her were her eyes. From the bottoms of the caverns of flesh and bone they flamed with a hard glitter that was almost feverish.

'Have you got that precious husband of mine safely under lock and key?' she demanded, addressing Mr. Budd; and when he nodded: 'I hope he'll hang! He deserves to hang! A thorough bad lot!' She went over to her favourite corner by the fireplace and said no more.

Pullman brought in the coffee, and while they were drinking it Gerald Trainor entered.

'Hello!' he said cheerfully. 'I'll have some of that.' He nodded towards the coffee tray. 'Well, so the mystery's solved, eh?'

'Very nearly, sir,' said Mr. Budd. 'There's one or two bits ter do. F'rinstance, we've still got to examine the contents of that safe.'

Trainor looked at him queerly. 'That's not going to be so easy,' he remarked, stirring his coffee.

'Oh, it won't be difficult, sir,' replied

the big man, 'once we get it at the Yard. I've got a man comin' down ter fetch it tomorrow mornin'.'

The other changed the subject, but several times while they were finishing their coffee Mr. Budd caught a thoughtful expression in his eyes.

Alice Devine departed soon after in Rutherford's car. Pullman brought down her numerous bags and hat-boxes, and she went without saying goodbye to anybody.

'Well, miss,' said the stout man, setting down his empty cup, 'I think we may as well be goin', too, now. I've locked the door of Curtis' room, and Inspector Tipman 'as got the key. A man 'ull be comin' ter collect his luggage, so I'd be glad if you would forward the front door key to me when you've finished with it.'

The woman agreed readily, and Mr. Budd and the sergeant took their leave. The big man's last sight of Wildcroft Manor was as he turned into the Mallington Road. He looked back and saw a thin, straight column of smoke rising from among the trees — the smoke from the expiring fire in the lounge.

* * *

Night covered the countryside. A black, starless night with low clouds that scurried silently before the wind. In the hollow, where lay the shadowy outline of the deserted house, there was no sound except for the faint sighing of the trees as they whispered ceaselessly in the breeze. All was still and silent, too, in the vicinity of the old inn. Beneath the lowering sky it sprawled, uninviting — empty. Far away over the open country came the soft sound of a train whistle; and then, at the end of the old post road, appeared a light.

At first it was only a mere pinpoint in the blackness, two tiny sparks that looked no bigger than cigarette-ends. But steadily they grew larger, and the hum of an engine broke the silence. Nearer and nearer to the black shape of the inn they came. A car with dimmed headlights loomed out of the night and stopped in front of the tumbledown entrance. The figure of a man slipped down from the driving seat and vanished in the shadow of the porch.

There was the sound of metal against

metal, a gentle click, and the protesting creak of hinges. The figure melted away into the darkness of the now-open door, and once again all was silence and blackness, except for the dim lights of the motionless car. And then, suddenly, a lurid glare lit up one of the broken windows. It flickered redly, died, flickered again, and grew steadily brighter. The figure of the motorist came running through the open doorway, looking backwards as he ran. Climbing into the car he started the engine, paused for a moment to stare at the fire he had started, and then drove swiftly away.

The red glare inside the old building changed to orange, and then to yellow. Fanned by the wind, the flames licked greedily at the rotting woodwork and ancient panelling, portraying their eagerness by a deep-throated roar that grew momentarily louder . . .

Billows of heavy black smoke coiled upwards, tossed hither and thither by the wind until they took on curious shapes — queer, distorted shapes that resembled the figures of old women dancing madly in the light of the flames. The glare lit up the trees on the fringe of Devil's Wood, tinging them with the colour of blood. The same ruddy light flecked the low, scudding rain clouds, and like a gigantic beacon, the Witches' Moon burned. The sparks flew in millions, chased upwards by snaking tongues of yellow flame. With a thundering crash the roof fell, and then —

An appalling explosion shook the ground and echoed over the countryside. Great flaming masses of burning debris were flung skywards and scattered to the wind. Long before dawn broke greyly, nothing remained of the old inn except a heap of hot stones and smoking embers that smouldered throughout the night and far into the coming day.

16

The Whole Truth

The following statement was made by Leslie Curtis in the presence of Superintendent Robert Budd, C.I.D., and taken down verbatim:

'My name is Leslie Andrew Curtis, and I am making this statement voluntarily and of my own free will, without coercion of any kind.

'I may as well say at once that I killed Hebert Marsh, John Krayle, and George Devine. I also killed James Augustus Dench, and hid his body in the tunnel at Seldon Cutting.

'The reason why I killed these men is easily explainable. I, and not Marsh, was the person responsible for blackmailing all the people concerned in this business. Marsh was as much a victim as any of them — in fact, it was only after I had been blackmailing him for some time that I first conceived the idea of extending the business to the others.

'Many years ago I discovered something about Marsh in connection with his brokers' business that would have rendered him liable to a long term of imprisonment, and so got him under my thumb. He had taken some money belonging to one of his clients, and he came to me to borrow the amount to put things right.

'He was quite frank about it, explaining the whole position, and I agreed to help him, provided he put what he had told me in writing and signed it. From that time onwards he had to do anything he was told. I found out about Devine — that he never wrote one line of his stories for himself, but paid a man in Brixton a miserable pittance to do it for him. I learned of Trainor's folly, and that Hope had been in prison. I discovered that Marsh's sister had contracted a marriage with her brother's chauffeur and was ashamed for it to be known, and afterwards I found out that this man was wanted for robbing his former employer, and obtained a hold over him, too.

'In order that I should not appear in the matter I made Marsh do the actual negotiations. I forced him to invite the people I selected down to his house, and made him pay all the money he got out of them into his bank. When I wanted any I went to him for it. There was nothing at all to connect me with the blackmailing business; in fact the others thought I was one of the victims as well — even his sister. Marsh kept all the documents, and if anything had gone wrong I was completely immune from any suspicion. This arrangement on my part was an error of judgement, as I shall show.

'Everything went well for a long time, and then Marsh began to show signs of kicking over the traces. I was pushing him too far, and one day he said that he was sick of it, and that, rather than go on with the plan, he would give himself up for what he had done and take his punishment. I knew that he meant what he said, and I prepared to make my plans accordingly.

'It was getting near the time for Marsh to issue the usual invitation to Wildcroft Manor, where the people had to pay up. I persuaded him to do this, saying that it would be for the last time, and that I would let up on the whole thing afterwards. It *was* the last time so far as he was concerned.

'To cut a long story short, during that weekend at Wildcroft Manor I shot Marsh, and then realised that he had been too clever for me after all. A long time before I had persuaded him to make a will in my favour, and this I had deposited with my bankers.

'After his death I took it out, only to discover that he had signed it in some kind of invisible ink, for where the signature should have been was nothing but a blank space. The money that was really mine, I couldn't touch — it all went to Cathleen, as next of kin. But that was not the worst. He had removed the safe in which he kept all the documents concerning the people I was blackmailing, and I had no idea what he had done with it. My stock-in-trade was gone — the evidence that I had acquired, with so much difficulty, was beyond my reach. The only thing I could congratulate myself on was that I had drawn a very large sum from Marsh on the previous day, but this was poor consolation for what I had lost. I think Marsh must have guessed I meant to kill him after his threat, and he took the course he did in order to have the last laugh.

'The police never suspected me of the crime, and the rest of the people who were at the manor thought it might be any one of them, since they all had a motive for killing the man who — as they believed — was blackmailing them.

'There was one person who, I know now, did suspect me. That was John Krayle. Circumstances have made me believe since that Marsh said something to Krayle during that visit. I'm sure that he mentioned the existence of the book and the verse, and hinted that it contained a clue to the hiding place of the papers which incriminated them all. Otherwise I don't see how Krayle could have realised its significance.

'Whether he also hinted that he was afraid of me, I don't know, but something made Krayle suspicious. He didn't say anything then, however, believing that if I had killed Marsh, I had killed him because he was blackmailing me. Nobody would have given the other away. That wasn't what was scaring them. What they were afraid of was that the police would find those documents that Marsh held. That's what I was afraid of, but for a different reason.

'When the police investigations were over and the house was shut up, I went down several times and searched it thoroughly. Since nothing had been found I concluded that Marsh must have hidden the safe in a very secure hiding-place. It used to be kept inside a sliding panel behind the head of his bed — the police didn't find that — but the space was empty. I thought there might be something of the same sort somewhere else.

'It took me a long time before I was certain that there wasn't. During my search I found the name and address of a man called Dench. It was scrawled roughly on a scrap of paper and had stuck behind one of the drawers in Marsh's desk. I had never heard of Dench, but I discovered, after a lot of trouble, that he was the retired employee of a firm of safe-makers. This set me thinking. I wondered if he knew anything about the missing safe. It was possible that Marsh might have employed him to move it somewhere.

'I couldn't go and just ask him, for the Marsh murder had created quite a sensation, and if I started making inquiries about a safe it might reach the ears of the police. I decided at last to kidnap him. I caught him one night when he came out to post a letter, gave him a shot of dope, and took him to the Witches' Moon in my car. It was the irony of fate that I should have chosen the very place in which Marsh had hidden the safe I was looking for. It's not so surprising, though, when you come to think of it. We were both looking for a good hiding place, and the old inn, with its bad reputation, offered the best in the district. Nobody ever went near the place.

'I had no intention of harming Dench. All I meant to do was to question him about the safe. He admitted that he had worked at the safe-makers, and that he had brought the safe to Wildcroft Manor in the first place and fixed it in the panel behind the bed, but he denied any knowledge of it beyond that.

'I thought he was lying, and I kept him at the Witches' Moon, trying to make him talk. I had taken care to cover my face with a handkerchief when I visited him, but one night this slipped, and that was why Dench had to die. I couldn't free him now, because he knew me. I killed him and took his body to the tunnel. I don't know why I didn't leave it at the inn. I had some idea that it would be better to put it somewhere that had no connection with me, I think.

'Then Cathleen Marsh issued her invitation. I was worried. I thought that the police had discovered something. In case of trouble I got hold of Harry Hutton. He had changed his name and was living in Camberwell, down and out. I knew that he and his sister weren't on speaking terms, and that Emily Marsh hadn't seen him for years — he left her when he found that he couldn't get hold of her money — and he was the only man who could carry out the plan I had in mind.

'I want it to be clearly understood that I had no intention of committing any more murders — Krayle's and Devine's were forced on me. All I wanted was to have someone on hand who might be useful in a tight corner.

'Mary Hutton and Pullman went to the manor a day before the rest, and Hutton and I saw them arrive. We waited for our opportunity until Pullman had gone into the village for supplies; and then, overpowering Mary, we took her to the old Mill, and Harry, as I had arranged, took her place.

'If Krayle hadn't hinted during that first evening that he knew I had been behind Marsh in the blackmail business, he would be alive now; but after that I had to kill him. I had been talking to him earlier while he was unpacking and I had seen the pistol he had brought.

'I took this during the evening, and when everybody had gone to bed I slipped along to his room. He opened the door when I whispered that I wanted to see him. I talked to him for a minute or two while he went on searching through his suitcase. I think he was looking for his pistol. Anyway, he was squatting by the case, and I thought that I might as well finish the business there and then. I pretended that I had heard something in the corridor and opened the door. When I was outside I turned and shot him, running back to my room as quickly as I could.

'I knew nothing about the book and

the verse then, nor should I have attached any importance to it if I had. It was only when I heard that it had been stolen that I guessed it might hold a clue to the whereabouts of the safe, or the papers. I saw you, Superintendent Budd, find the book by the coal-box, and during the night I went to your room and got it — I had watched where you put it through the keyhole.

'But the flyleaf had been torn out. There was nothing else in the book, and to get rid of it, I put it back on the table in Krayle's room. I was coming away when I saw Devine approaching. I watched him go into the room I had just left and come out carrying the helmet. It puzzled me to know why he had taken the thing, and I followed him back to his room, and watched him through the keyhole.

'I saw him comparing the helmet with a slip of paper, and then I heard voices downstairs and had to hurry back to my own room. But I didn't go to bed. I was certain that Devine had found the secret to the safe. Krayle must have taken him partly into his confidence about the verse and its relation to the helmet, and it was this which made me certain that Marsh told Krayle something before he died. I was determined to get the secret out of him.

'Just before dawn I heard somebody pass my door, and looking out saw Devine, fully dressed, creeping towards the staircase. I went after him and tackled him in the hall. He told me that he had found where Marsh had hidden the papers, but he wouldn't say where it was. I had to stop him finding those papers. I had no idea what Marsh might have put with them — what reference to me, I mean. That was one of the things that had worried me all along — that Marsh might have left an account of our relationship. I stabbed Devine and, after I had searched him and found nothing, I hid the body in the ottoman, and went back to my room.

'I was still no nearer my object — the discovery of what Marsh had done with that safe — and I was trying to decide what steps I should take next, when you found it at the Witches' Moon. That gave me another shock. I got hold of Hutton and we tried to remove the safe, but you turned up unexpectedly and very nearly caught us both. By this time I was beginning to get desperate, and I planned to kidnap Cathleen and hold her hostage. I realise now that this was a mistake, for it was really the means of leading you to the discovery of Hutton, and through him, me. If I'd left well alone the police would never have combed the country and found that mill.

'I think that's all. I played for big stakes and I lost — it's the luck of the game, I suppose.

'(Signed) Leslie Andrew Curtis.

'(Witness) Robert Budd, Superintendent, C.I.D.

'(Witness) A. Branscombe, Detective-Sergeant, C.I.D.'

'What about this 'ere safe of Krayle's?' said Leek, when the statement was read to him. 'He doesn't say anything about that.'

'I don't think it ever existed,' grunted Mr. Budd. 'You tried every possible place with a photograph of Krayle, didn't yer?'

The sergeant nodded. 'Yes,' he said sadly, 'I walked me feet into blisters tryin' ter find it.'

'An' yer didn't,' remarked the big man, 'because there was nuthin' ter find.'

'But what about Devine's letter?' demanded Leek. 'That said Krayle 'ad a safe deposit somewhere.'

'I've bin thinkin' about that,' interrupted Mr. Budd, 'an' I don't think Devine meant a word of what he said in that letter. It was just ter put us off. He knew that Miss Marsh 'ud show it to me. The safe he was after was at the Witches' Moon.'

'Maybe you're right,' said the sergeant, and then musingly: 'Queer how that place caught on fire.'

'It's not queer at all,' retorted Mr. Budd. 'Trainor stayed behind at Mallington after the others had come to town. An' he didn't leave until the followin' mornin'. I'm not sayin' any more. We'll just leave it at that. It's my opinion that that safe was better destroyed. It'll set a lot o' people's minds at rest, an' none of its contents is needed as evidence. Personally, I think that fire was a bit of very good luck — or, maybe, of judgement.'

THE END

THE FACELESS ONES
GRIM DEATH
MURDER IN MANUSCRIPT
THE GLASS ARROW
THE THIRD KEY
THE ROYAL FLUSH MURDERS
THE SQUEALER
MR. WHIPPLE EXPLAINS
THE SEVEN CLUES
THE CHAINED MAN
THE HOUSE OF THE GOAT
THE FOOTBALL POOL MURDERS
THE HAND OF FEAR
THE SORCERER'S HOUSE
THE HANGMAN
THE CON MAN
MISTER BIG
THE JOCKEY
THE SILVER HORSESHOE
THE TUDOR GARDEN MYSTERY
THE SHOW MUST GO ON
SINISTER HOUSE & OTHER STORIES

We do hope that you have enjoyed reading this large print book.

Did you know that all of our titles are available for purchase?

We publish a wide range of high quality large print books including:
Romances, Mysteries, Classics
General Fiction
Non Fiction and Westerns

Special interest titles available in large print are:
The Little Oxford Dictionary
Music Book, Song Book
Hymn Book, Service Book

Also available from us courtesy of Oxford University Press:
Young Readers' Dictionary
(large print edition)
Young Readers' Thesaurus
(large print edition)

For further information or a free brochure, please contact us at:
Ulverscroft Large Print Books Ltd.,
The Green, Bradgate Road, Anstey,
Leicester, LE7 7FU, England.
Tel: (00 44) **0116 236 4325**
Fax: (00 44) **0116 234 0205**

Other titles in the
Linford Mystery Library:

THE WHITE LILY MURDER

Victor Rousseau

When New York department store magnate Cyrus Embrich is found stabbed to death at his office desk, the police have little evidence to go on. Embrich's secretary reveals that her employer had been in fear of his life, and in the event of anything happening to him, he had asked her to call in the famed private investigator 'Probability' Jones to assist the police. Aided — and at times led — by his able assistant Rosanna Beach, Jones finds himself caught up in the most complex and dangerous case of his career . . .

FIRE ON THE MOON

V. J. Banis

On vacation at her Aunt's villa in Portugal, Jennifer is attracted to both Neil and Philip Alenquer, two brothers who live in an old castle overlooking the sea. But Jennifer soon senses that something is wrong, though it is not clear where the intangible clues are leading. Words left unsaid; the burnt-out shell of a cottage; terror in response to the recitation of a poem; gunshots on the beach. It is a mystery with potentially deadly consequences, as Jennifer and her aunt learn when an arsonist sets the villa alight . . .

SINISTER HOUSE & OTHER STORIES

Gerald Verner

Whispering Beeches stands vacant, well back from the roadway, almost hidden by the thickly growing trees that give it its name — though since its owner, Doctor Shard, was murdered by an unknown hand three years ago, it has locally been known as Sinister House. One night, noticing a light in one room, newspaper reporter Anthony Gale enters through the open front door — only to stumble over a man's body lying stark and rigid, with a gaping throat wound! Four tales of mystery and the macabre from veteran writer Gerald Verner.

FATAL FLOWERS

V. J. Banis

'I saw a chauffeur hit a girl and knock her unconscious. Then he threw her into a limousine and sped away . . . ' Alice Whelan finds horror on Falcon Island: home of her retired movie star mother, Diana Hamilton, and her sixth husband, Leland Braddock. Who is the mysterious girl locked away in the mansion's tower? What is the truth behind the elaborate greenhouse that Leland and his brother maintain in the nearby woods? And what strange experiments are the two conducting with their Fatal Flowers?

THE DARK CORNERS & OTHER STORIES

Robert J. Tilley

A schoolboy disappears — but the missing child may not be all he seemed . . . A mortician and his family find their new neighbours disturbingly interested in their affairs . . . Quiet Mr. Wooller finds himself the only man ready to take down the Devil . . . An escaped convict stumbles upon an apparently idyllic holiday cottage . . . A spouses' golf game ends in murder . . . In an outwardly perfect marriage, one partner is making dark dealings . . . A young man is subjected to a bizarre hostage-taking . . . Seven unsettling stories from the pen of Robert J. Tilley.

THE SYMBOL SEEKERS

A. A. Glynn

In 1867 a box treasured by a distin-
guished American exile in England is
stolen. Three battle-hardened ex-Southern
soldiers from the recently ended American Civil War arrive on an unusual
mission: two go on a hectic pursuit of
the box in Liverpool and London, whilst
third takes a path that could lead to
the gallows. Detective Septimus Dacers
and Roberta Van Trask, the daughter
of an American diplomat, risk their
lives as they attempt to foil a grotesque
scheme that could cause war between
Britain and the United States . . .